1985

"CHARM AND ENERGY. . . . A BRI....
TERWOVEN MULTIPLE NARRATIVE."   *—Time*

Martha Grimes
The Deer Leap

"Full of grace, wit and verve, aided by a host of memorable characters. Solid work from one of the best in the genre."   *—Kirkus Reviews*

"The spirit of Christie, Allingham, and Sayers lives on."
                                         —Los Angeles Times

"A superior writer . . . *The Deer Leap* is deft . . . amusing and worthy of Martha Grimes's generally admired series."   —Newgate Callendar,
                         The New York Times Book Review

"A writer to relish."   *—The New Yorker*

"Her wit sparkles, her plots intrigue, and her characters are absolutely unforgettable."   *—The Denver Post*

By Martha Grimes

THE MAN WITH A LOAD OF MISCHIEF
THE OLD FOX DECEIV'D
THE ANODYNE NECKLACE
THE DIRTY DUCK
JERUSALEM INN
HELP THE POOR STRUGGLER
THE DEER LEAP

The Deer Leap

by

Martha Grimes

A DELL BOOK

Published by
Dell Publishing Co., Inc.
1 Dag Hammarskjold Plaza
New York, New York 10017

The poetry quoted throughout this book is by Emily Dickinson.

Dell ® TM 681510, Dell Publishing Co., Inc.

ISBN: 0-440-11938-3

Reprinted by arrangement with Little, Brown and Company, Inc.

Printed in the United States of America

November 1986

10 9 8 7 6 5 4 3 2 1

WFH

to the memory of my father

Was it a pleasant Day to die —
And did the Sunshine face His way —

Contents

A Wounded *Deer* — *leaps highest* —
I've heard the Hunter tell —
'Tis but the Ecstasy of death —
And then the Brake is still!

The
Deer Leap

PART 1

Good Night!

Which put the Candle out?

One

Una Quick had been searching for two days for her dog, Pepper.

Whenever anyone in Ashdown Dean came into the post-office stores (of which Una had been purveyor of goods and stamps for forty-five years) she would ask the same questions over and over, thereby delaying the dispensing of letters, tinned goods, and half-loaves for as long as she could keep the benighted villager's attention. Everyone in Ashdown knew Pepper's habits in tedious detail.

"Probably just run off or someone picked him up. And don't forget that lab," added Sebastian Grimsdale with his usual compassion. Over the two torturous days, Sebastian finely tuned this theme with references to dog- and catnapping, never forgetting to toss in references to the Rumford Laboratory, where, according to Mr. Grimsdale, they did all sorts of dreadful experiments. Having reduced Una Quick to tears, he would then tell her not to worry, and leave with his post and tinned tomato soup. This he would later reduce to something slightly thicker than water but considerably thinner than blood for the guests of Gun Lodge.

Blood was, indeed, his milieu: Sebastian Grimsdale was Master of Foxhounds and Harriers and his own huntsman. The only persons he actually paid were his one maid-of-all-work, and his head keeper, Donaldson. Donaldson was a great stalker. Like most of them, from Scotland. But Grimsdale preferred Exmoor, the game being much larger. That was through now until spring, damnation. This put Grimsdale in an even more insufferable mood than was usual for him. He was cheered only by the thought of the meet in five days — though running a fox to ground was no comparison to the stag at bay. Well, in the meantime, he could take his shotgun out to the pond and see what flew by. . . .

With poor Una Quick clutching at her heart — she had a "heart," as she described her condition — most of the Ashdown villagers offered far gentler and happier prognoses. "Pepper'll be back, you'll see, dear," said her neighbor, Ida Dotrice. "You know the way they are. Just turn up at the door like always. . . ."

Una was not sure the way they were after going missing for two days.

Little Mrs. Ashley, whose baby sat with its moon-face half covered by a cloud of white blanket, consoled Una by telling her the tale of "those dogs and that cat that went for hundreds of miles, or something, and finally got home." Mrs. Ashley panted slightly, as if she had just made the journey herself, while shoving marmite and bread into her carryall. She went on about these animals: ". . . all the way from Scotland or somewhere, I don't remember. Didn't you read it? Well, you ought, one was a Siamese, you know how smart they are. . . . How much do I owe? Oh, that much. Things get dearer every day. And what they charge for just *dog* food. . . . Oh, sorry, Miss Quick. You must get that book." She could not remember its name. "Don't you worry now. Ta."

Siamese cats trekking through Scotland did not console

Una Quick at all. She grew paler with every chime of the steeple bell that reminded her that everyone would pass to his reward, including Pepper. The vicar, a tiny man who walked as if he had springs on his shoes, had not helped Una with references to all of us going to our reward.

On the third day, she found Pepper. The liver-spotted dog lay stiff as a board in the tiny shed behind her cottage where she kept her few gardening supplies, one of them weed killer. The door had been secured, she was positive, by a stick driven through the metal clasp.

Una collapsed. Ida Dotrice, come to ask to use her telephone, found and revived her. Una was barely alive.

It was the first time the post-office stores had been closed during the week, other than half-day, when Pepper's funeral was held in the backyard of Arbor Cottage. Una, wearing black, was supported by Ida and her other neighbor, Mrs. Thring. The vicar had been persuaded to read over the small grave, and he did this, but somewhat springily.

Paul Fleming, the local veterinarian and the assistant administrator of the Rumford Laboratory, had said, yes, it was undoubtedly the weed killer. Una asked him how Pepper had managed to work the stick out of the latch. But Una was known to be slightly absentminded. Paul Fleming had shrugged and said nothing.

✕

The Potter sisters — Muriel and Sissy — were well known in Ashdown Dean, largely because hardly anyone knew them at all. They were famous for keeping their shades drawn, their doors locked, and themselves behind them. Groceries were delivered by a local boy, and there was never any post. When they did appear, one was always dressed in black and one in mauve, as if in the first and second stages of Victorian mourning. It was considered an event when they had gone up the High Street to the Briarpatch tearoom to sample the proprietor's famous pastries.

After all of these years of shuttered living, the Potter sisters were seen leaving their house the day after Pepper had died, their cat wrapped in a blanket, and getting into their ancient Morris.

Sissy drove hell for leather up the street and out of town, where Dr. Fleming's office was situated.

They returned without the cat and locked the door.

✠

Gerald Jenks, a surly man who kept a cycle shop on the edge of the village, also kept a spitz as surly as Gerald himself. The dog was chained to a post outside the run-down shop like a guard dog. What there was to guard, no one knew. Only Gerald could have found anything of value in the tottering stacks of wheels and parts and pieces.

The day after the Potter sisters' cat had died from a heavy dose of aspirin, Jenks found the dog caught in a rusty bicycle chain, its efforts to escape apparently having strangled it.

If it hadn't seemed impossible, one would have thought the animal population of Ashdown Dean was methodically killing itself off. Or being killed.

✠

Una Quick lay in bed three days later, not having risen since the funeral. Stiff as adamantine, hands clasped over her bosom, a votive candle burning beside her.

The vicar hadn't wanted to read the service over Pepper, she was sure. Beneath him. *Him.* Fidgety old fool, he was. Some just didn't understand how you got attached to an animal.

Here in her tiny cottage in Aunt Nancy's Lane — two up and two down — she'd nursed a crotchety mother for twenty years. And forty-five years keeping the post-office stores. Little enough thanks had she got from the villagers for *that*. Selling soup and sorting post. So what if she had her bit of fun with it. That taint of perfume on letters to Paul Fleming. Handsome, thought he was God's gift.

The candle guttered in a tiny gust of wind. She had held one at the funeral, and when that went out she had lit another and then another. Keeping watch. In that breeze she smelled a storm coming. Una thought of it waiting out there, like Death.

When the steel band gripped her below the breast, she winced. The beat of her heart was uneven and ragged as her breath. Dr. Farnsworth had come and gone directly after the funeral to check on her again. Would he be annoyed if she called him on the Monday? Tonight? Instead of Tuesday?

The band loosened and the constriction eased. No, she mustn't fall prey to the habit of some patients. He had laughed, pleasantly enough, his arm round her shoulder, and told her to stop dwelling on her heart, as it only made matters worse. But it had almost killed her this time, what with Pepper's passing away. Arsenic. It must have been horrible. . . .

Across the room the telephone rang, and she wondered if she should make the effort. It persisted. She dug her feet into slippers and went to it.

The voice was strange. Strangled, almost.

The message was stranger.

She wiped beads of perspiration from a brow cold as pearl.

Two

Ordinarily a person who could be rendered speechless by the public in general, Polly Praed was ready to strangle the woman in the public call box. At least she thought it was a woman; it was hard to tell in the rain pouring down the call box, drenching Polly's yellow slicker, water flung like sea-spray against her eyes. A sudden beak of lightning turned the blood-red box a livid yellow, but the damned fool just nattered on.

Had she not been *in extremis*, Polly Praed would no more have thought of pounding on the glass of the door than she would have considered giving a speech at the annual Booker Award ceremonies. Not that she'd ever get the chance. The trees that lined the High Street could have accepted the award better than Polly Praed. Ten minutes now. Ten minutes. She wanted to scream.

Unfortunately, screaming was out, too. She had failed her est course in London. When commanded to fall on the floor and scream, she had sat like a rock.

She had failed her Assertiveness Training course in Hertford, too.

Any call from her editor threw her into paroxysms of fright; he would call to "check on her progress." In his sly, friendly way.

About the only people she could manage were a few of her friends in Littlebourne, and she was cursing herself for a fool for not staying there in the first place.

The rain poured, the lightning clawed, and that odious man at Gun Lodge had had the nerve to tell her the Lodge telephone was for private use only and directed her up this hill to the call box.

She felt like throwing herself against it, toppling the damned thing and the person inside who must be calling everyone in Ashdown Dean. Fortunately, it was a tiny village. Probably only another twenty calls to go.

If her editor hadn't phoned her to "check on progress," she'd never have set off on this harebrained literary excursion in the first place. Canterbury first, then Rye, as if the imaginations of Chaucer and James might fall at her feet like cathedral stones or tiles off roofs. Then up to Chawton and Jane Austen. Not even Jane could make the wheels start turning.

Had she stuck with Assertiveness Training, she would simply have told that Grimsdale person — *demanded* — that she must use his telephone. Then, of course, the storm hadn't risen to gale force. So she had trekked up here.

Raining cats and dogs.

She wouldn't have minded if it had rained down her own cat, Barney. That dreadful person said no animals allowed. Barney was used to the car, having made this literary pilgrimage with her. And she had gone sneaking out after dark to bundle him in.

Only Barney wasn't there.

If she hadn't got kicked out of est, she would have been able to go to police, rout out whoever was around. But she knew, instead, who to call and who would give her advice, since he had been so free with advice over the last two years whether she wanted it or not.

Finally, in a furor, Polly put her hand in the metal pull and yanked the door open.

"I'm *sorry!* It's an *emergency!*"

The woman responded quickly enough. She fell backward across Polly Praed's feet. Her hand was still holding the receiver and the cord lay snakelike, half in, half out of the call box, as the lightning knifed again and showed a waxen face.

It was too much like her stories to be believed.

Here she sat in the police station on a hard chair waiting for Constable Pasco to come back. Polly, having done a great deal of research in the course of writing her mystery novels, knew that rigor mortis had either passed off or not yet started in the body whose head had used her feet as its cushion. Having gingerly removed those feet, she had had no choice then but to step over the elderly woman and ring up the local police. The lonely public telephone in the rain had quickly become a carnival of whirling blue lights and villagers materializing out of Ashdown Dean's cottages and narrow streets.

For a good twenty minutes she had been sitting on this chair, waiting. Since Constable Pasco was the single local policeman, he had sent to some town five miles on another edge of the New Forest for reinforcements. Polly had been surrounded at the call box, questioned, plunked down here.

And no one cared about Barney. She told herself not to worry. Barney had probably just crawled out the window. Barney wore a red neckerchief and would have got the gold medal in Assertiveness Training. . . .

Literary inspiration. Good God.

She was absolutely stuck for a plot and she had that contract staring her in the face, promising January delivery of a book that she hadn't even started. And it was October twenty-second. All the way from Canterbury to Battle she'd contrived a plot around six people in a first-class train compartment making bets on which of them could tell the most interesting story before they got to their destination. She had been killing them off one by one as each had to leave for the toilet or somewhere. She didn't know who was doing the killing or why . . . the Chaucer scholar, perhaps, who had thought it up.

Battle had scratched that plot when she saw the Battle Rolls in the Abbey and wondered if a murder incorporating William the Conqueror might not be instructive. But think of all that research. . . .

Then Rye. Henry James. Inside Lamb House she wondered how a mystery in which several people have achingly endless, convoluted conversations over tea and biscuits, all of them knowing there *was* that body in the solarium but, with their Jamesian sensibilities, making such oblique references that no one knew if anyone knew if he or she knew. Including the reader. Her fascination with the endless possibilities of this grew. It would break new ground in the mystery world. A mystery within a mystery. A cobweb-covered windowpane. Her editor wouldn't know what was going on, but would of course have to pretend he did, being a man of Jamesian sensibility himself.

But her hopes were dashed when she picked up *The Awkward Age* and tried reading it over tea and cakes and realized that, although she couldn't make head nor tail of it, Henry James probably knew what he was doing. Damn the man!

Why hadn't she stayed in Rye for dinner at the Mermaid, as she'd been tempted to do? Or spent that extra day in Canterbury? Or never left Littlebourne, where she would be just settling down in bed with somebody else's mystery, hoping there might be something she could nick?

Thus did Polly Praed, like a film running backward, retrace her movements over the last three days. After leaving

Jane Austen's imagination in Hampshire (where she now was), Polly had planned to motor along and make a casual stopover in Long Piddleton, Northamptonshire, though she didn't see how one could merely be straying by the family seat of the Earls of Caverness. Well, he kept *asking* her to visit, didn't he?

Half an hour. No police. Constable Pasco had questioned her quite thoroughly and, she thought, with some suspicion. Why hadn't she used the telephone at Gun Lodge? Because that Grimsdale person wouldn't *let* her.

Finally, he came in, and she found a sliver of steel in her spine, enough to say, "I'm allowed one call."

Feeling a fool for all of the times she'd heard that on American television programs, she blushed. Pasco, a tall, laconic policeman, merely plunked the telephone on the counter and told her to go ahead, miss.

Pleased at least by the *miss* — Polly had left her "miss" days behind her like a string of pop beads — she picked up the receiver. If he was so plentiful with advice and succor, let him advise and succor his way out of *this* mess.

In this way, Polly Praed decided to dump the whole thing on the former Lord Ardry, eighth Earl of Caverness, pretty much like she dumped her hastily written books on an unsuspecting public.

PART 2

What Inn is this
Where for the night
Peculiar Traveler comes?

Three

"*T*ime!*" called Dick Scroggs.

The publican of the Jack and Hammer called for last rounds at ten. The deference he showed his occasional overnight guest was absent with his regulars, not even bothering with the *please* or the *ladies and gentlemen* to announce the closing hour.

Considering the lack of variety of ladies and gentlemen, all but one of whom were gathered at a table in a small bay window, Dick might be forgiven his abruptness.

Marshall Trueblood, who lent what variety there was, glanced at his watch and called back to Dick, "Isn't it a bit early, old sweat? It's only just gone ten. Since when did you start locking up before the half-hour? Let's have another round, anyway." Marshall Trueblood nodded in the direction of Mrs. Withersby, asleep by the fire. A pistol shot wouldn't have bestirred her faster than a shot of gin.

"Of course, *you* needn't worry," said Lady Ardry to her nephew, Melrose Plant.

Melrose Plant lowered his crossword puzzle and raised his eyebrows. The comment had come, unhooked to previous conversation, a tail without a dog. She had been rustling the financial pages of the London *Times*, having put by the *Telegraph.*

Lady Ardry's presence here at this latish hour was testimony to all that the dregs of the beer, of the day, and most probably of the autumn had been reached. She could generally be counted on to turn up here or at Ardry End throughout the day, but she had always stoutly announced that for her, morning was at seven. She was no layabout, like others. Always in bed by ten.

"About what needn't I worry, dear aunt?" He did not wait upon her answer: the comment had been loaded, he was sure.

"Funds, Plant, funds. Investments. Money. About which you needn't worry, not with *your* inheritance."

He did not bother to answer. That the seventh Earl of Caverness, his father, had not left at least one wing of Ardry End to his sister-in-law Agatha would forever put Melrose Plant in the company of rogues and bounders. Nor did she seem to recall that Melrose's father had left her provision in the form of a cottage in Plague Alley and an annual allowance. She must have been squirreling it away, though, considering the high teas she consumed at Ardry End, family seat of the Caverness line.

"I want something safe for one. Something that will allow me capital gains should I decide to sell. Something that will not fluctuate with rising and falling markets. Something absolutely stable." She drank her shooting sherry. "I'm considering precious metals. What do you suggest?"

"The Holy Grail," said Melrose.

"Antiques, old trout," suggested Marshall Trueblood, Long Piddleton's single dealer in them. "I've a fine jade dragon, Ming Dynasty — give a century, take a century — that I'll let go cheap — to you." He flashed her a smile and lit up a pink Sobranie. As usual the cigarette was an extension of the costume. Trueblood was wearing a safari jacket, a flamingo neckerchief and a chartreuse shirt. On the table was a panama hat. In October. Left over from Guy Fawkes Day, perhaps. Melrose calculated that Trueblood could clear the jungle just by stepping out of the bush.

"You could buy my house," said Vivian Rivington to Agatha.

"*That* old falling-down place? You've left it go too long, Vivian."

Trueblood snorted. "Falling down? It's the handsomest cottage in Long Pidd, and you know it." He turned to Vivian. "But really Viv-viv, you do keep putting it up for grabs and then taking it off the market."

Melrose could not stand this absurd chatter over his aunt's "investment potential" a second longer. The only thing Agatha would ever invest was time — a large part of it spent before her nephew's fireplace consuming tea and cakes. He slapped his checkbook open, uncapped a thin gold pen. "What do you want for it, Vivian?"

Vivian Rivington looked from him to the checkbook and said, in a small voice, "Whatever are you talking about, Melrose? *You* don't want my house."

"True. But at least you'd have it sold, and then you wouldn't always have to be zipping back and forth between Northants and Venice." He smiled obligingly. "Sixty thousand. Seventy? We could avoid all the rigmarole of estate agents, et cetera." The pen was poised over the checkbook, calling her bluff.

She cleared her throat. "Well . . . it's not *certain* I want to sell. . . . I mean, Franco's been talking about keeping the place. For a bit of a holiday now and then . . ."

Melrose returned pen and checkbook to pockets. "Count Franco Dracula will find Long Piddleton bereft of nubile maidens or convenient crypts in which to stuff them —"

The usually quiet Vivian flared. "I *told* you to stop calling him that."

"Yes, really, Melrose," said Trueblood. "Viv's looking absolutely grand since she got back. Not pale at all."

Her hazel eyes flashed Trueblood a warning, too. "Both of you make me sick." She started to wrap her terribly de la Renta scarflike thing about her, preparatory to rising.

Trueblood was right: she did look quite different whenever she returned from Italy — but it was a difference Melrose could have done without. He suspected the fiancé (who'd been hanging on for some time now) had a good deal to do with her highlighted, upswept hair, her lacquered nails, her fashion-plate clothes. Why was that crushed-leather belt, for instance, riding down somewhere round her hips? Melrose sighed. It would take a couple of weeks to get her back into the old Vivian-rut of twin-sets and nice, shiny, shoulder-length hair.

"Oh, sit down, for heaven's sake," he said crossly.

She sat. "Dick's closing up, anyway."

"Well, he'll have to deal with Withers, first."

Mrs. Withersby, although her longevity in the Jack and Hammer might have earned her the sobriquet, could not be called a pillar of the pub. At the moment she was sprawled across the hearth, out cold.

Scroggs, who seemed to have forgotten his call to arms of nearly a half-hour ago, was holding out the telephone receiver. "For you, m'lord," he shouted across to Melrose Plant.

Plant frowned. "Me? At this hour . . . ?" It would be Ruthven, he thought. Ardry End, like Manderley, must be burning.

ⅹ

The connection was dreadful. Cracklings all along the line, as if someone had indeed sent out the fire brigade.

It was a trunk call, much to his surprise.

More to his surprise, from *Polly Praed.* He could not believe *she* was calling *him.* "What are you talking about, Polly? You fell out of a call box?"

On her end, Polly Praed wanted to throttle him. *"No! I didn't fall out, she* did . . . no, no, no!" As if Melrose could see as well as hear across the miles, she shook her dark curls in a frenzy. "I wasn't *in* the call box with her, you idiot!"

Melrose smiled. "Idiot" was a backhanded compliment. Melrose seemed to be the only adult this pathologically shy woman could confront. Around children, animals, and the Natural World, she did well. He had first met her in her village of Littlebourne, in colloquy with a tree. "Look, this line is awful. Can you hear me?"

"Enough of you."

He wondered what that meant.

She spaced her words out carefully, as one does when talking with the demented. "This woman just fell *over* me."

"Where are you?"

Irritated beyond belief, she squeezed her eyes shut. She'd told him twice. Through clenched teeth, she spelled it: "A-S-H-D-O-W-N-D-E-A-N. Borders the New Forest. They won't let me leave —"

When Constable Pasco turned a questioning glance on her, she slid down the counter, putting the telephone on her lap, and whispered.

"Did police *tell* you she was murdered?"

"Well, good Lord, what else could she be?"

"Try to be calm, Polly. Now, I take it you want me to come straightaway."

"If you like."

If he liked. How gracious. The New Forest was over a hundred miles away.

"I was just thinking . . ." Polly sat there on the station floor, winding the telephone cord round her finger.

Silence.

"You were just thinking," said Melrose, "that I could get Superintendent Jury down there." Under pain of death, Polly could never have called Richard Jury herself, though she knew him well enough. "No." Melrose had to hold the receiver away from his ear.

When she was through yelling, he brought it back. "Jury has probably the usual mess of pottage on his platter — rapes, murders, thefts — and, anyway, he couldn't go to Hampshire without a formal request from that constabulary, which I doubt will be forthcoming."

Silence again on her end. He sighed. "Polly. Have you *any* idea what happened?"

"Yes," she snapped. "The lady didn't pay her bill and Telecom did her in!"

Smash went the receiver in Ashdown Dean.

four

etective Superintendent Richard Jury was not, on
that same evening, working on a case and might have
welcomed an interruption of the little seduction
scene taking place in the bed-sit directly above his own flat.

Carole-anne Palutski (a.k.a. Glo Dee Vine, her "stage"
name), whom he had first met a month ago when she was
wrestling an armchair up the narrow steps of the Islington
terrace house, was bending down to a minuscule table for a
couple of bottles of Carlsberg, gyrating her Sassoon jeans
with a toss or two not absolutely necessary for the task at
hand. On one of the rear pockets was an appliquéd *Smartass*,
and when she turned, Operation Carlsberg successfully com-
pleted, the little heart appliquéd on the crotch fairly
throbbed. Carole-anne believed in advertising fore and aft.

"Want an Elephant, love?"

Since she was holding up the Carlsberg, she meant beer.
Jury wondered what the answer would have been from someone with less restraint — or not old enough to be her father,
as Jury certainly was. Twenty-two was what she said she was.

He let it pass, mentally ringing up nineteen. "One more and I'll run downstairs like Niagara," he said. "You look a little wobbly yourself, Carole-anne."

She lifted a skintight-jeaned leg. "It's only the shoes, love. Four-inch heels these ones must be. And call me 'Glo,' " she said, probably for the umpteenth time that evening.

"No. It doesn't suit you."

Carole-anne pouted and set about decapping the Carlsberg in such a way the beer foamed over and ran down the tank top that didn't need anything more to let him know how little lay between thin cotton and skin.

"Now look what I've gone and done," she said wonderingly, as if she hadn't for a minute meant to go and do it. Beer was snaking down her naked torso to the jeans. Where the "waistline" was supposed to be, only Sassoon knew: it seemed to ride her pelvis at the moment, the belt holders threaded with some silky stuff that ended in little balls cavorting with the red heart.

"Come here," said Jury, who was seated on the lumpy daybed.

The false lashes lowered over deep blue eyes, her whole expression saying *at last.* She swayed over to him, still holding the beer bottle, and landing the viscous torso right in front of his mouth.

Jury took out his handkerchief and wiped her stomach.

Her mouth fell open and her arms fell down, clutching the bottles as if she'd wring their necks. He took one from her and swigged it.

The empty hand went to her thrust-out hip. "Well, ain't you a hoot and a scream, then? You can't be queer, so what's the argy? I mean, I ain't exactly an old dripper."

"Not since I wiped the beer off." Jury smiled.

Her face went red and he thought she was going to yell, but instead she fell down on the bed giggling. "Takes all kinds." She sighed and leaned her head on his shoulder. "You're my first failure."

"Maybe I'm your first success."

All she did was screw her face up and look at him as if he must be crazy.

"Men are thick on the ground, Carole-anne. You know what I'd do if you were my daughter?"

"Nah. What?"

"Kick your little Smartass right across the room. Maybe buy you some Gloria Vanderbilt jeans — at least the swan's harmless — and a cashmere sweater. Loose."

"You like kinky sex? That it?"

Jury put his forehead against the Carlsberg and laughed. That was the only way she could look at anything.

"Well, I was only trying to pay you back," she said. "You know, for helping me with the furniture and all that."

"For God's sake, Carole-anne, can't a man help you without your having to go to bed with him?"

She thought that over while she picked at the bottle label. Carole-anne shrugged. "Tits for tat."

ⅺ

The odd-lot furniture hadn't taken a removal van to bring it, just a lad driving an old pickup. Her earthly possessions were vested largely in herself. She was gorgeous. Navy blue eyes, waist-length hair, a shape that would show through potato sacks. He'd helped her stow the furniture, turn the tiny bed-sit into some sort of home, and then taken her out to one of the locals for a bite.

On that warm-for-September moving day, she'd been wearing bright blue sateen shorts, cut up above the line where buttocks met legs, and over this, as if for modesty, a short skirt of the same material. The modesty was very mild, however, since the skirt was slit up both sides, thereby emphasizing the legwork underneath rather than hiding it. The weather hadn't been *that* warm, but he doubted Carole-anne dealt much in coats.

Whether you started at the floppy sandals and worked your way up, or at the spaghetti straps of the cut-off blouse and worked your way down, the effect on the men at the bar was unanimous. Heads moved in a synchronized turn that would have done a chorus line proud.

Studying the chalked specials on the little blackboard at the serving bar, Carole-anne didn't give the starers and hopeful-gropers a second thought. "Cottage pie, couple of Scotch eggs, chips, salad." Then when she saw Jury was ordering sausages, she added, "And one of them ones, too." She left Jury to see to the filling of the plate and slapped her sandals over to a little table, stuffed next to a banquette. Moses parting the Red Sea couldn't have made more space than this vision in blue sateen.

"You're a *what?*" said Jury, halfway into his sausage, watching Carole-anne stuffing in cottage pie.

"You needn't get huffy. A topless dancer." She shrugged a shoulder in some unidentifiable direction. "Over to King Arthur's. Never been?"

"That sweatshop? Only when I was nicking one of the dips that works the passage."

"You? A superintendent? Lower yourself, don't you?"

"This one's a personal friend. Listen, you shouldn't be doing stuff like that. What in hell would your parents think? They probably don't know."

"Listen to him, would you?" She appeared to be addressing the Scotch egg. "Mum's dead. And Da—" She shrugged. "Who knows? Anyway, I can't even remember him." She said it matter-of-factly.

"I'm sorry. But you must have *some* family."

Her deep blue eyes looked up, slightly puzzled. "Why? There's lots don't. Do you?"

"Not much of a one. A cousin. Lives in Newcastle. How've you been getting by, Carole-anne?"

Again, those blue eyes regarded him, this time with a sparkle. "You kiddin'?"

Jury said nothing.

She sighed. "Oh, okay. I'm not into that. What I want to be is a dancer or actress."

"Thought you were one," he said.

"God, you're wors'n a dozen mums. I mean a *real* actress. Tried out for *Chorus Line*. Almost got a part, too."

"Well, if you didn't, the casting director must have a Seeing-Eye dog."

She hesitated and then laughed. "Thanks."

"That's your ambition, then? West End musicals?"

"West-bloody-End musicals? Well, it'd do for a start. What I'm really good at is the straight stuff. You know. Like that Judith Anderson or Shirley MacLaine, maybe."

"You sweep the board, that's for sure. Had any lessons?"

"Some. Need a bit of training." Her look was quite serious as she scrutinized her Scotch egg.

"A little, at least. I've got to get to work. I'll see you back to the house. I'm keeping an eye on you, Carole-anne."

Shrugging a creamy shoulder toward the bar, she said, "So what else is new?"

‰

"Polly? Polly *Praed*? In a phone booth — ?" Jury had left Carole-anne's flat after checking the dead-bolt lock and fixing the loose chain. ("*You going to bolt me in, Super?*")

Just as he entered his own flat, the phone rang. He wasn't on rota, so it shouldn't be New Scotland Yard, but, knowing his chief superintendent's tendency to ignore who was first, second, third down, he fully expected one of Racer's late-night calls-to-arms. That didn't mean anything was happening in criminal London that demanded Jury's attention, only that Racer's club and the pubs were closed.

So Jury was pleasantly surprised to hear the voice of his old friend Melrose Plant on the other end.

"Sure, I'm working on a case. Racer makes certain my hands are either full or tied behind my back. Where is this place?"

Jury wrote it down. "Okay. What else did she tell you? . . . Hmm. Well, you must bring out the best in her." Jury smiled. "I'll see you there tomorrow. Unofficially, that is. The Hampshire police wouldn't appreciate my coming along uninvited."

Hung up on him, had she? Jury shook his head, looked at the dull paperwork in his hand, tossed it back on the desk. From his memory of Polly Praed, getting her to talk about anything at all was like being stuck at a party of clams. She struck him as extremely shy, unless the subject got around to murder.

five

Una Quick, according to Dr. Farnsworth, had died of cardiac arrest.

It was the storm and Ida Dotrice's account of Una's habit of calling her doctor, who signed the death certificate, that provided the Hampshire police with a reason for the accident. Dr. Farnsworth, whose practice was in the nearby town of Selby, examined Una Quick every month, like clockwork. It was unfortunate (Farnsworth had told police) that Miss Quick had not had a clockwork heart. Could go at any time.

Una had told Ida Dotrice that Dr. Farnsworth insisted she call him once a week — every Tuesday after office hours to report on her condition. How the latest medication was affecting her, or how the old ticker was doing, or whether she'd been going against his orders and drinking more than her limit of two cups of tea, and so forth.

But the storm Tuesday evening had brought down a telephone line and she hadn't been able to ring up the doctor from her cottage. So she had stupidly taken the walk up that hilly High Street to the call box dutifully to report to the doctor.

The call had never gone through; Una had passed out in the kiosk and instead of slumping to the floor, as one might have suspected, she'd been supported by the telephone box itself. Must have thrown her arm across it — as police reconstructed the case — to keep from falling.

Dr. Farnsworth did not appreciate the irony of his patient's death put down to a gradual but nonetheless steep climb to a call box to report on the state of her health.

⊁

It was morning and Barney was still missing.

Melrose Plant would be here at any moment. Now, of course, she was hideously embarrassed that she'd got him all the way down here to Hampshire under false pretenses. Perhaps she could suggest they take a nice drive through the New Forest or have lunch somewhere. Or something. Polly scrunched down in her chair in the dining room of Gun Lodge.

Why she felt perfectly comfortable talking to *him* — he who was, or had been, one of the Earls of Caverness, and Viscounts Somebody, and a baron, and who knew what else, and had given it all *up* . . . Polly knifed the table mat as if it were one of the defunct titles. Not that she gave a fig for a title. She simply disliked people acting in a way contrary to what she would have them doing in her books. Earls and dukes and marquesses were supposed to stay that way.

"Ma'am," said a spindly girl who seemed as shy as Polly herself. The girl had waited at table last night, had brought her early tea this morning, and seemed to be the only employee in Gun Lodge. She deposited a bowl on the table.

"What's that?" asked Polly, peering into the bowl.

"Porridge, ma'am," said this pathetic breath of a girl, who then scurried away.

Polly had no appetite anyway. Not with Barney gone.

The girl was back. *Go away,* she thought with the embarrassment of one who doesn't want to be caught crying. "A gentleman to see you, ma'am."

She looked down, listened to the approaching footsteps, said a brief (and rather surly) *Good morning* to Melrose Plant's *Good morning, Polly,* and without preamble, told him: "Coronary occlusion, that idiot doctor said. Well, maybe it was, but why was she in that call box anyway?"

Melrose Plant put his silver-knobbed stick on the table, sat down, and said, simply, "I don't know. Why're you crying?"

"I'm not," said Polly, his obvious sympathy breaking a logjam of tears, which now flowed freely. "My cat's missing."

"Barney?"

That was the trouble with him. He even remembered the name of her cat. Not only that, but he seemed more interested in her cat than that she'd got him here on a wildgoose chase. She wiped her face with her napkin. Why he seemed actually to *admire* her was beyond her comprehension. She was off-hand, rude, demanding, and temperamental. "You're a masochist," she said, sniffling.

"Obviously," said Melrose, looking at the bowl. "So must you be if you're eating that." He took a spoon and stuck it in the porridge. It stood there.

"Don't touch it. You may never get back to Ardry End. I was met at the door by a gray-mustached, dreadful man who seemed to want a full accounting of my life before he'd rent me a room."

"Why did you stay, then? There's a perfectly good little pub with rooms a bit farther along."

Polly looked up, enraged. "He told me there *wasn't* any other place."

Looking round at the prison-gray walls, the plastic placemats, the porridge, Melrose said, "How else could he get custom? Never mind. You can have my room at the pub and I'll stay here."

"I can't. See, Barney might come looking for me."

Remembering Barney's battle scars, more likely he was out looking for a leopard to fight.

"Don't worry. We'll find Barney."

He was rewarded with a deep look from Polly's violet eyes. That he had been dragged all the way from Northampton-shire to Hampshire was nothing in the light of eyes like amethysts. The rest of her was ordinary enough. But who would bother looking at the rest of her? Melrose had to look away. "I take it you are thanking me?"

She churned the spoon in the awful gruel and more or less shrugged, dropping her glasses back in place. They often rode on her head. "Thanks."

"Ah, the bliss! The everlasting gratitude! The hundred-mile drive — !"

"*Do* stop being dramatic. You know you've nothing much to do."

"How gracious. Except find your cat." She deserved to be humbled a bit. "Well, not to worry. I called Superintendent Jury. He should be showing up in —" Melrose paused for a bit of drama with his gold watch "— in an hour or two."

Medusa couldn't have done a better job of turning some-one to stone than did the eyes of Polly Praed, now a stormy purple, staring into the green ones of Melrose Plant. "*What?*"

"Why are you looking at me as if I'd just marshaled the Coldstream Guards? *You* were the one who hung up because you were so blasted angry I wouldn't call him. So, I called him." Melrose poured himself a cup of lukewarm tea and asked if she minded if he smoked. From her look, he could have gone up in flames, and no one the sorrier. "Look, I *did* what you wanted."

"Well, *this* is just wonderful. The poor woman keeled over from a coronary. But she didn't keel, that was the trouble.

There I was, thinking it was a live person making a call —"

"Not an unreasonable assumption. But you mean this is why I'm here?" He could see that her mind was somewhere on the A204 tracking Jury's car. Melrose might have been dragged from his own deathbed — that wouldn't worry her.

"How am I going to explain to Superintendent Jury that I'm not up on a murder charge — ?"

"The way you're pointing that knife, you soon might be." He moved the blade away. "I don't know," he said, smiling wonderfully. "Poor Jury. Dragged all the way from London on a missing cat case —"

Polly Praed slapped her napkin on the table and slid down in her seat, still staring at or through him.

Then she said, to his surprise, "Why didn't she have an umbrella?"

PART 3

Children—swindled for the first
All Swindlers—be—infer—

Six

She wore a washed-out blue denim pinafore over a white jumper, sneakers faded like the denim, and no socks. Her hair was nearly platinum in the slant of sun breaking through the drizzling rain and the trees that surrounded Ashdown Heath. The shine of her hair made up for the lack of light in her face, a pale oval, glazed with rain. Her eyes were the same wash blue, faded like the rest of her. She looked like any other ordinary fifteen-year-old, except for the .412 shotgun butted against her shoulder, as she squinted along the barrel at the two boys thirty feet away.

"Put the cat down," she said.

Billy and Batty Crowley had been stopped in the act of pouring the can of petrol on the ginger cat. It had a red bandanna round its neck and looked almost like a cartoon cat — eyes white and huge with terror, fur sticking out like pine needles. Batty Crowley was just about to strike a kitchen match.

She had walked softly up behind them, a quarter of the way across the heath, and they'd been so absorbed in their game they hadn't heard her until she'd said it: "Put the cat down."

They turned and stared at her, their own eyes frozen over now like the cat's. When they didn't react as fast as she liked, she cocked the gun and snicked the safety.

Then she said: "Take your shirts and sweaters off."

They looked at each other and then back at her as if she were the mad one who'd contrived the merciless game in the first place. "What the bloody hell you mean?"

"Take your shirts and sweaters off. Now! Wipe that petrol off with the shirts."

Both of them, each holding a leg of the squirming animal, bellowed with laughter —

Until she fired. She fired into the dirt of the cleared-off place where they were going to barbecue the cat. They ripped off shirts and sweaters and started wiping the cat down. They were sweating, half naked in the cold of the October morning.

"You're —" screamed Billy Crowley. He must have thought better of telling her what she was when he saw the shotgun come up slowly, aimed somewhere in the area of his forehead.

"You got the petrol off?"

They nodded, squatting down and wiping for all they were worth. The cat screeched and clawed Billy.

"Wrap those sweaters round the cat so it can't lick itself and put it in that box you brought it in." When she motioned with the shotgun, they cringed. "Bring the box here."

"What — ?"

The gun moved again; the question went unasked. It would certainly have gone unanswered.

Billy wrapped the sweaters around the cat and stuffed it — screeching and clawing — back into the box.

"Here."

They did as commanded, setting the box about six feet

from her. Rustlings and bumpings came from the box that
looked as if it were moving by itself, a trick box.

"Now you just run like hell across the heath and I'll just
stand here till I can't see you any longer."

They didn't look back.

She didn't wait. She broke the gun, took out the other shell
and dumped it with the box of them in her pocket. Then she
picked up the cat, hid the gun in some bracken, and ran
through the trees until she reached the road that led out of
Ashdown Dean. Where she ran even faster.

Seven

Polly Praed was still staring malevolently at Melrose Plant three-quarters of an hour later when he had moved them from the dining room of Gun Lodge to the more pungent airs of the Deer Leap. Since Melrose had taken a room here, the publican, John MacBride, was only too happy to open the bar at ten.

"It's a point, certainly. No one would have gone out in that storm without an umbrella." He looked around at the chintz-covered cushions of the chairs and window seats, the windows once again lashed with rain; at the inglenook fireplace; the pewter and brass mugs hanging above the bar; the copy of Landseer's painting of a stag hanging above the fireplace. "But I'm not sure what it means."

Neither was Polly, so she switched the subject. "That Grimsdale person nearly shut the door in my face for even suggesting the Lodge wasn't the Ritz."

"Um. Well, don't worry too much about your predicament. I expect the superintendent can clear you when he gets here."

"That's so funny I can hardly contain myself. I'd like another Guinness." She shoved her half-pint toward him, former earl, present lackey.

Melrose pretended not to hear her and looked at his watch. "He should be here any time now."

Forgetting her Guinness, Polly started collecting her umbrella. She was still wearing that yellow mac and hat. "Give him my regards."

"If you think you're leaving after all of the trouble you've caused, you're quite wrong. Anyway, my dear Polly, it's too late."

Melrose watched her die a thousand deaths and knew exactly what was in her mind — she sat there in that ridiculous oversized hat and mac, gum boots to match, looking as if all she needed was a small boat and a large net and she might come back with a crocodile.

Actually, he rather enjoyed her dilemma, even if he couldn't say he enjoyed the reason for it. Polly was absolutely gaga over Jury, but Melrose was intelligent enough to know that gagaism didn't add up to love.

He leaned across the table and whispered, "Don't you remember that love means never having to say you're sorry?"

"Having some trouble, are you, Polly?" asked Jury, after he'd greeted Melrose Plant. He and Detective Sergeant Alfred Wiggins pulled out chairs and sat down. Wiggins smiled and blew his nose by way of hellos all round.

Melrose looked at the stag in the painting, both of them mere innocent bystanders.

Turning her glass round and round, she managed to get out a strangled "Yes."

Melrose watched as she tried to outmaneuver conversational possibilities. To him, she had detailed the odyssey of her journey round the Kentish coast and up through Chawton like Ulysses. Now, of course, she was tongue-tied.

Jury waited. Nothing doing. Ectoplasm in a yellow slicker.

He cued her: "You found this body in a public call box, or at least that's all I could get out of Mr. Plant."

Melrose sighed and looked up at the stag. The innocent always suffered. He turned to Wiggins. "How are you, Sergeant?"

Wiggins merely shook his head. "Caught a chill. It's pneumonia weather. Runs hot and cold. And the rain doesn't help."

"Quite right," said Melrose. "It's hell."

"Wet hell, sir." Wiggins said he was going to the bar for a buttered rum. Would the superintendent care for anything?

"Pint of bitter, thanks. Miss Praed — Polly?" She might have been out like a light. "Tell me exactly what happened."

"What happened? Well — didn't *he* tell you?"

Jury smiled, and Plant thought he should have known better. The smile only made her shrink further into her slicker.

"Okay. I'll tell you what I know and you supply the missing details —"

"Barney." She looked down into her empty glass. "Is a missing detail."

"Your cat."

Quickly, obliquely, she ventured a glance from under her brim. "You remembered."

"Your cat? Who'd forget him? I think I'd be afraid more for anyone who crosses his path. Go on."

"No, you."

Good heavens, thought Melrose, sighing hugely, they might have been playing Patience. That was certainly Jury's game. Why didn't he simply reach across the table and shake her till her teeth rattled — dragging him all the way from London. But no, he would never lay a hand on a woman; he would just sit there with that damned smile . . . no wonder they melted at his feet.

As now. "Okay. You opened the door of the call box and an elderly woman fell at your feet. That sum it up?"

She beamed. "Perfectly. But she didn't have an umbrella."

Jury looked puzzled. "That significant?"

Polly raised her eyes to heaven. "It was *raining*."

"Good heavens, Polly," said Melrose. "I wouldn't take that tone with the superintendent, here."

The eyes dropped as Wiggins returned with Jury's drink and went back for his own, which he had to wait for, since he wanted it medicinally hot.

"That *is* odd. Good for you, Polly. . . ."

Jury's voice purred on. He might have been petting that damned moth-eaten cat of hers. It really wasn't fair, thought Melrose; *he* had gone to all of the trouble —

"Oh, sorry, sir," said Sergeant Wiggins, breaking the spell of those violet eyes riveted on Jury's gray ones.

"Hmm?"

"Your glass, Mr. Plant. Let me get you another." His racking cough was somewhat more convincing than Polly's little throat-clearings. But then Wiggins had had years of practice. He looked at Plant's empty bottle of Old Peculier and shook his head, frowning slightly. "I'd suggest a nice hot buttered rum, sir. Never seen such weather. Ran straight into the eye of a storm coming here —"

He would turn it into a monsoon. "Just some more Old Peculier, thanks."

As Wiggins slouched off (still in coat and muffler), Polly was becoming slightly more voluble, probably hypnotized by the gray eyes. Anyway, it was either talk or burn.

Plant just sat there turning his small cigar round in his mouth. She hadn't arrived at the doctor's report yet. Thus far, the only criminal activity was the catnapped Barney.

Under other circumstances, Jury might have appreciated Polly's epic, himself being a lover of Virgil, but even the superintendent's patience had its limits. He was already into his second pint when he finally asked the Fatal Question: "How was she murdered, then?" When Polly simply studied her hands, Jury asked, "What did the medical examiner say?"

An indrawn breath. "Well, this woman wasn't *exactly* murdered."

Jury looked at her. Wiggins looked at her. Plant studied the picture. Neither the stag nor Polly had a chance.

It was Wiggins who finally said, "Not 'exactly.' Could you explain that, miss?"

Polly blew out her cheeks. "Yes. Well, it more or less looks like she died of some kind of heart-thing."

Melrose offered helpfully: "There wasn't a knife or a bullet in the heart, Superintendent. Not that sort of heart-thing."

That got him a gum boot in his shin.

"Coronary?" asked Jury, his expression bland.

Polly nodded and nodded, bobbing her dark curls. She had, during her tiresome exposition, at least removed her ridiculous hat.

There was rather a lengthy silence as Polly slowly scraped at a dried bit of food on the tabletop.

Melrose, eyes narrowed, watched Jury watching Polly. There it was, that damned slow smile. Instead of beating her about the shoulders with a table leg as she deserved, she having hauled him — or, worse, gotten Melrose Plant to do her dirty work — all the way from New Scotland Yard where there would be hell to pay when he got back . . .

"Not to worry," said Superintendent Jury. "You never know. It sounds pretty strange; police might be jumping to conclusions. . . ."

Vigorously, she nodded. "That's just what I said."

She'd said nothing of the kind.

"And Barney missing." Now she slumped back, tearful.

"We'll find him." And then, hemming in that smile, quite

deliberately, Plant knew, Jury said to *him*, "But really you should have got more of the facts before you called. . . ."

Polly's smile at Jury was dazzling.

Melrose shut his eyes. Why didn't they just stuff him and mount him like a deer?

Eight

Paul Fleming's surgery was a half-mile outside Ashdown Dean, along the road which Carrie had just
run, the cat sliding back and forth like a boulder in
the cardboard box.

She watched Dr. Fleming, who was, unfortunately for him
(Carrie thought), the village "catch." He took the cat out of
the box. Wrestled it out, rather. The cat in the red bandanna
wasn't looking with any more kindness on this second helpful
member of the crew than he had on her. As the veterinarian
more or less tossed and held it on the examining table, she
wondered if animals, like humans, remembered their tortur-
ers and could go after them later, for she surely would like to
set this cat on the trail of Batty and Billy Crowley.

Paul Fleming was sniffing the air. "Where'd you find this
one? Smells like it's been dumped in a petrol pump."

Carrie scratched at her elbows. She never believed in giving out any more information than absolutely necessary. Constable Pasco would be bad enough, and she intended to get to

him before the Crowley boys' aunt did; that way she might get off with the usual lecture, instead of jail.

"It has been. Someone put petrol on it. I got off what I could but I didn't know —" She shrugged.

She held the cat steady while he got soap and water. "How long's it been? I mean since you found it?"

"Fifteen minutes maybe. Just soap?" She nodded toward the pan of water.

"Castile. Beef fat. The petrol defats the skin. You wrapped the sweaters round him?"

Holding the cat still, she merely nodded.

Fleming looked from cat to Carrie. "To keep him from licking at the petrol? That was smart. Apparently, it didn't get any in its system; I'd hardly call this cat lethargic." The cat took a swipe at the towel. "Hold on, you big thug. Two sweaters. You must've been cold." He glanced up at her.

No reply.

"Where'd you find him?"

"On the heath."

"Well, what the hell was he doing running round out *there?*"

"*I* don't know, do I?"

Her refusal to give out the details had nothing to do with wanting to protect the Crowley boys. She wished they'd burn in hell. In petrol, in hell. Carrie simply didn't believe in telling any more than she had to. Not even to Dr. Fleming, whom she supposed she could stand being around for ten minutes at a time, which was saying a lot for someone who walked on two feet. But she didn't approve of his work at the Rumford Lab. She never lost a chance to remind him of that.

"Off work, today, are you?"

He looked at her. "You don't call this 'work'?"

Carrie looked at him. "I mean from the lab."

Fleming looked as if he was just barely controlling himself. "Let's not have another go at that, if you don't mind."

"The RCVS doesn't seem to be doing much to improve things." She rolled her eyes ceilingward to avoid looking into his. "I mean, they change the language around and so forth. 'Termination condition.' That's pretty good. Why don't you say what you mean?"

Paul Fleming glared at her. "Listen, if there wasn't any animal experimentation, what about this cat here? That ever occur to you?"

She looked at the big tom. "I guess it's a point."

"Thanks!"

"Kill fifty cats to save one." Slowly she nodded. "It's a point."

"You do *not* know what you're talking about! God! Why aren't you up there with the rest of the demonstrators, torching away?"

"It's against my principles."

He looked at her and shook his head.

Carrie knew it upset him, just having her walk in. Too bad. He was pretty nice. And Gillian Kendall was probably in love with him.

Poor Gillian. Carrie watched him as he worked and had to admit he was handsome, also good with animals, also unmarried. He'd be better off to stay that way, and so would Gillian. Carrie was a reader, and was constantly amazed at how few books could get by without the Big Love Scene. These scenes neither embarrassed nor repulsed her; she merely found herself grandiosely indifferent to the intermingling of lips and bodies. It was their unlucky lot to be caught up in a fate worse than death.

"Instead of standing there mooning, help me," he said, handing her a towel.

"I never moon." She wiped the cat.

"Bring in a jaguar next time, will you?"

Carrié liked the way the cat's pupils spurted in the light like red-hot coals, probably a reflection up from his red bandanna.

"God, is that a *smile* I see?" he asked, wiping the cat's fur down.

Quickly, she erased whatever giveaway look had been there. She hadn't known he'd been watching her.

"Gone," he said, sighing heavily. "Well. I guess you'll live, tiger."

That the cat would not only live but probably outlive them both was clear. It wrestled with Fleming as if they were both on the mat and then flung itself on the floor.

"Oh, for heaven's sake," said Carrie, picking him up and plunking him back in the box. "You got one of those cardboard cat-carriers?"

He sighed. "You're already into me for three of those. One pound apiece."

From her pinafore she pulled some pound notes and slapped three on the table.

Paul Fleming reddened. "Look, it's okay —"

"I robbed Nat West."

"All right, all right, don't give me that stormy look." From a low shelf he pulled out the cat-carrier and unfolded it, handles upright. He smiled again. "Ten pounds is the usual fee. But for you —"

"That all you think about? Money? You know I'll pay you."

Again, he smiled. "Just a penny. For your thoughts. What *do* you think about, Carrie?"

She picked up the carrier, just as much of a boulder, but quieter. "Fates worse than death. Thank you." She walked out.

ᴐ

Too late.

Police Constable Pasco slammed down the telephone and glared at her, so she knew Amanda Crowley had already rung up. Probably the reason it took Amanda so long was because she knew Billy and Batty were guilty. "I'm reporting a crime," Carrie said.

"That so?" Pasco folded his arms across his chest and plunked his feet up on his desk.

"Batty and Billy Crowley got hold of a cat and were going to burn it." She put the cat carrier on the ledge between his desk and the tiny entryway. "Here he is."

Pasco pointed to the telephone. "*That* was Amanda Crowley on the phone just now. She said you aimed a gun at those kids."

"What was I supposed to do? Let them burn up the cat?"

"This is the eighth time —" He looked up at a huge calendar with pictures of grazing sheep on it. Carrie wondered why he'd want to look at sheep or cows or anything else on four feet. He didn't care about animals. "No, tenth — *tenth* time — you listening?"

"Yes." She lowered her eyes as though in sorrow and shame but actually to look at the copy of a manual put out by the RSPCA on his desk. The constable must have been doing his homework. He kept count on the calendar of how many times she'd been in here on some complaint from a villager.

"Well, you better, Carrie. Just because you got the protection of the Baroness —"

That, thought Carrie, *was a giggle.*

"— doesn't mean you can go round untying dogs, stealing cats —"

"If you mean Mr. Geeson's beagle, he kept it on a chain morning and night and that's against the law." She held up the blue manual, slapped it back down.

His blue eyes narrowed. "*It's against the law to threaten people's lives!* This is the last time —"

"You want the fumes of roast cat ponging through the village?"

He closed his eyes, pained. "Don't think I'm not on to you. Don't think I don't know who unstopped earths during cubbing season. If I get one more complaint from Grimsdale —"

She tuned him out. Sebastian Grimsdale was Master of Foxhounds and Harriers, one of the shining stars in the Ashdown Dean social heavens.

Disgust stamped on his face, Pasco drew a pad toward him. "What's its name?"

Carrie frowned. "The cat's? Batty didn't introduce us —"

"Smart." He pointed the pen like an arrow at her. "Fifteen and so damned starchy you probably sleep standing up. What's it look like, then?"

"See for yourself. He has a red bandanna round his neck. He doesn't live in Ashdown Dean —"

He told her to keep the thing *inside* the box. Then he swiveled in his chair and picked up the phone. As he dialed he said, "Know every cat and dog and pig and fox in town — Hello?" He asked for someone named Prad, it sounded like. He left a message they'd found her cat.

"The cat belongs to a guest at the Lodge. One of these days, Carrie, big, big trouble —"

Again, she lowered her eyes. "Yes." She picked up the carrier.

"Leave it here," commanded Pasco.

"Finders, keepers," she said, running out the door with the carrier before he could go for his gun.

☒

As she walked past the blue sign with the white *P* that told all of Ashdown's villagers where to find help, Carrie reflected that, taken all in all, her relationship with Constable Pasco wasn't so bad. She'd certainly been in his company often enough to know.

⊠

Coming along the walk toward her was Donaldson, Sebastian Grimsdale's head keeper. He was a Scot, supposed to be a brilliant stalker and harborer, and she loathed him. How he could have lowered himself to come here and help Grimsdale with his bagged and kenneled foxes, Carrie couldn't imagine. And another supposedly good-looking one with his copper hair and square face. Carrie had heard he was having an affair with Sally MacBride, the publican's wife of only a year.

"Ah, and if it isn't wee Carrie."

Wee Carrie, indeed. She could have slugged him.

He stood directly in her path and when she tried to get round him he did a sidestep first one way and then another. She refused to ask him to let her pass. Carrie simply stood her ground and stared straight through him. There were times when she honestly thought slime like Donaldson was not solid, that she could reach out and stick her hand right through him. If he was soulless, why wouldn't he be bodyless?

His smile was one of the most unnatural, one of the most twisted she'd ever seen. He made a grab for the carrier, which she moved quickly out of reach, behind her.

Looking her up and down in what was supposed to pass for a lazy, sexy glance, he said, "Y' should do yerself up proper, lass; y'd be a looker."

Still she said nothing nor did she move.

"Got nowt to wear but that damned faded pinafore? It hides too much." His own eyes stared at her breasts, or what he could see of them, their bloom deliberately obscured by the sweater and shapeless pinafore.

Of course, he was trying as hard as he could to unsettle her, to make her nervous, to make her strike back. She just stood and stared.

"Aye, and I can stand here all day if needs be."

Carrie said nothing. He wouldn't have the patience to stop here another minute, if she knew him.

She did. Now disdaining her, he said, "Think y'r really the princess, don't ye? Just because you live with that old nut, the Baroness." Then he shouldered Carrie out of the way as if the pavement weren't big enough for the both of them.

As she kept on toward Gun Lodge, she thought of how different he was around Sebastian Grimsdale, M.F.H. Donaldson was like toffee. You could hardly get him off your fingers, he was so sticky-nice.

Sebastian Grimsdale was one of the Baroness's favorite guests, not because she liked him; she liked his posturing. He was forever at her silly *salons,* the most prominent of her guests — at least, in his own eyes. In Carrie's he didn't even reflect.

She was walking along the riverside that skirted the village, and came to the old playhouse behind the Deer Leap. The pub was built of chequers of local stone and knapped flint and had been simply a pub, until John MacBride's new wife decided to open up a room for paying guests and call it an inn. Sally MacBride was another one Carrie had no time for. She wouldn't let her niece have any pets at all. Carrie had thought of a way around that.

They didn't use the child's playhouse much anymore. It was awfully small and had no windows, but it had been fun when Carrie was younger. There were gardens at the rear of the inn, even an herb garden with peppermint and pennyroyal. Lupines nearly as tall as Carrie herself, roses, daisies, and all the rest "clumped" (said the Baroness) "all together with no respect for design, pattern, nor grace of movement."

Carrie could not quite understand why a garden was only good for the thought of oneself moving through it, but the Baroness probably imagined nothing else. In her own mind she would see herself by one of her reflecting pools; or walking with her parasol beneath an arbor of white roses; or reclining "gracefully" upon one of the many benches of white-painted iron. Carrie had once found her outstretched beside the privet hedge, drunk as three lords. It was nice to enjoy one's surroundings, she supposed.

The cat had been so quiet, she looked into the carrier to see if he was all right. He was peacefully dozing. Despite Dr. Fleming's care, you never knew. Turn around and you might find something dead. Besides: she did not understand how a veterinarian, who was supposed to be in the business of taking care of animals and saving their lives, could have anything to do with the Rumford Laboratory.

The laboratory lay over a mile from Ashdown Dean, a long low gray fortress surrounded by a chain-link fence. Carrie saw it as a long scar on a blighted field.

There had been demonstrations; she had walked there to watch them. But she didn't participate. The lab had been torched once by the Animal Freedom Front, and she couldn't for the life of her figure out their reasoning, since several rabbits had died from smoke inhalation. That aside, burning things down that you didn't like was against her principles.

Walking on to Gun Lodge, she kicked up the fallen leaves, wishing she could make a great pile of them and dive straight in. Cover herself up and lie there hiding for a while. Her arm was wearying with the weight of the cat, and there was an old oak tree by the river, one that looked as if it had been lightning-struck. It hadn't; there was a natural division that made a space just large enough to shove a small length of board into. She had found some wood to fit it and she liked to sit in the tree.

Although she knew she should get the cat back to the guest, she was awfully tired from the morning's work. So she put the carrier on the ground and sat down, drawing her legs

up with her sneakers against one part of the trunk and her
back against the other. The sunlight that in September had
filtered through the leaves had weakened to cast pale rivulets
across her legs. *And did the Sunshine face His way?*

Carrie twisted her face and flattened it against the tree
bark to keep from crying. Childhood amnesia. Her mother
and father were probably dead, but she would never know.

That was a line of poetry from somewhere. Carrie had
been to an East End school off and on, mostly off, and hated
it. What she knew she'd taught herself. She did not go to
school now. When social services came round to find out
why, the Baroness had told them Gillian Kendall was her
tutor (which she wasn't — she was the secretary), and when
threatened, the Baroness had counterthreatened with a verve
and energy that could only come from the fourth drink of the
afternoon. They always said they'd be back, but there were
no return trips.

The Baroness might be a little nutty, at that. That was fine
with Carrie, because all of the sane people she'd known
hadn't been God's gift.

Getting down from her tree perch, she picked up the box,
and once again looked up at the hazy sunlight, the sky like
pearl. *Was it a pleasant Day to die — And did the Sunshine
face His way?*

She squeezed her eyes shut. In a hasty moment, she had
even had to name herself and had no idea why she came up
with Carrie Fleet.

Nine

Sebastian Grimsdale stood at the window of Gun Lodge, his hands clasped, or, rather, wrenching themselves behind his back, watching her come around the stables. This morning when he had awoken at six, all had been covered with hoarfrost, dew frozen on each dying blade of grass, and he had known a moment of rare exhilaration. Hunting was the only thing that brought that on. Certainly the girl coming across the court didn't. Nor did that Proud woman. No, Prad. Something like that. And here came the Fleet girl carting the damned cat. Police, mind you! Had they nothing better to do with their time than go about the countryside looking for cats?

"I assumed Barney could stay in my room —" the Prad woman had had nerve enough to say.

Well, he'd scotched *that* plan mighty quick. Told her she'd have to leave the cat in the car, and when she'd turned to find lodgings elsewhere — nearly flung down the pen, rude woman — he'd taken thought about the eight pounds and told her the veterinarian could board the cat. The woman had seemed easy enough to subdue.

A cough behind him turned Mr. Grimsdale from the window to confront two of his guests. Archway, or something like. And his bleached-blond-haired wife who looked enough of a floozy to be in some West End musical. There she was now, dabbing lip-rouge on. Wondered how the husband, who had a face like a biscuit and wore rimless glasses, ever wound up with *her*.

He dragged his eyes away from her frontage, which was ample, and said, "Yes, Mr. Archway? What is it?"

"Archer. We were just wanting to pay our bill."

They were supposed to have stayed another night. Wasn't it awful enough that lean circumstances had forced him to turn Gun Lodge into a guesthouse (he refused to refer to it as a B&B) without those guests breaking their promises. "It was my understanding you were to stay two nights. *Two.*" The indictment made the husband redden, but the woman snapped shut her compact and said in her dreadful East End accent, "That room's as cold as a virgin's —"

Fortunately for her, the husband silenced her. An elbow in the side. Well, if they insisted on being difficult . . . "Checking-out time is at noon. It is now one o'clock." A long case clock in the entryway bonged the fatal hour.

And as if in tune with the sounds of doom, the giant iron knocker was raised and lowered once with a deadly crash. That Fleet girl. No respect for anything. "I am sure that you would not wish to pay for a night's lodging without the privilege of using it. No one has complained about the heat before," (actually, quite a few complaints along those lines had reached his ear) and here he sighed wearily — "however, I shall see Midge puts an extra heater in your room. Now, if you will excuse me."

Carrie Fleet stood on the wide doorstep and looked without expression into the eyes, hard as knuckles, of Sebastian Grimsdale. "I've come with the lady's cat."

There was a movement from within the box.

Grimsdale looked at both of them with the same disdain. "Just leave it."

"Here on the doorstep?"

"*I* will see she gets it."

Carrie, who seldom registered emotion, allowed herself the luxury of hating Sebastian Grimsdale, not only because she found him personally hateful, but doubly so because of his being Master of Foxhounds and taking the greatest pleasure in hunting anything (within the law) on the wing or on four feet — pheasant, rabbit, deer, grouse. Indeed, the only time she ever noticed him smiling was when he was tramping along with a gun in his hands.

"No," said Carrie.

"No? No what?"

"*I'll* see she gets it." Her tone was merely determined, but the major would take it as rank insolence. His face turned beet red. "Can't I come in and wait? I'll sit in the kitchen." If he let her in at all, she knew that's where she'd have to sit, anyway.

He glared at her, nodded curtly, and told her to go round back and Cook would let her in.

The delivery boy's entrance was okay with Carrie. She took the cat around to the back of the house, a big ramshackle brick place with a stone wall encircling it like an iron band.

When Polly Praed and Melrose Plant walked into the big kitchen of Gun Lodge, Carrie Fleet was drinking tea from a mug and Barney, out of his box, was dozing peacefully by the hearth. The cook, Mrs. Linley, had paid no more attention to the rules smartly laid down by Sebastian Grimsdale than did anyone else in Ashdown Dean: the greengrocer, the butcher, the librarian.

Polly rushed to the hearth and gathered up the intractable Barney, who seemed to prefer to sleep rather than be found. Barney had never been putty in Polly's hands. It was a bit embarrassing the way he squirmed to get back down to the tattered little rug on which he'd been toasting himself at Carrie's feet.

Polly momentarily put him down and said to Carrie, "Wherever did you find him?"

"On the heath." She shrugged. "It's near where I live. I guess he got out of your car and just wandered around."

"How can I thank you —?" Polly, with the aid of Melrose's handkerchief, wiped her eyes and blew her nose, which then looked frostbitten. She scrabbled about in her handbag, drew out her purse, and held out some folded notes.

Carrie frowned slightly. "I don't take rewards for stuff like that. It's against my principles." She put down her mug and got up.

Melrose Plant had been about to take out his wallet when she said that. The frown disappeared like a shadow's sudden passing and her face took on a lunar quality, something rather above it all, the expression calm as a nun's, though he felt there was something very unnunlike in its placidity. He had to admit here was someone under thirty who held a certain interest for him. He looked at his wallet, and turned back to see her pale blue eyes look quickly away from him. "That's certainly very kind of you."

Barney was again in a death struggle in Polly's arms, not impressed with the great reunion scenario. "He smells funny— well, soapy, or something." Polly sniffed the cat's fur.

"That's the vet's soap. Dr. Fleming. You can pay him if you want."

"A veterinarian? Was he hurt?" Polly started inspecting Barney, who let out an ungrateful growl and managed to struggle down to the hearthrug.

Carrie Fleet seemed to be considering. "No. But I didn't know whose cat it was; except for the bandanna, it could have been a stray. You don't have tags on him."

There was a definite reproach in that word *tags*.

"So I thought it'd be a good idea to take him to Dr. Fleming."

The girl was chewing her lip, and her quicksilver glance from the one to the other of them suggested to Melrose that there might be more to her story than she was saying. But he let it pass.

"But — well, that was so *good* of you. What's your name, then?"

"Carrie Fleet." She brushed the pale hair back across her shoulder and started for the door.

Polly Praed didn't know what to do about Carrie Fleet. "Where do you live? In Ashdown?"

Carrie Fleet turned. "Yes. With the Baroness."

And with that as explanation, she walked out the door.

ⅺ

As Carrie walked back along Ashdown's High Street, she realized how stupid her story had been and that the lady would go to Dr. Fleming and find out about the petrol.

Maybe a stranger's going to Constable Pasco and complaining would finally convince him that Batty and Billy were holy terrors around anything that couldn't defend itself. Maybe Batty couldn't help it, being the way he was, but Billy ought to be in borstal.

A family of ducks rowed up to the edge of the pond, probably hoping for lunch, seeing her there. But she had no bread today. She turned out her pockets in mute explanation, but the ducks didn't take the hint, and bobbed there, shoving one another about, each wanting to be first.

"No crumbs," said Carrie. "I can't *always* have crumbs, can I?"

She remembered Batty had been here one day, tossing in
pieces of bread, and when the ducks came up close to the
edge, he'd tried hitting at them with a stick until he saw Carrie and started backing off. She grabbed the stick and gave
him a small whack across his bum, just the thing his aunt
should have done. Even though she hadn't hit him hard, this
assault had landed her yet once again in front of P.C. Pasco,
being lectured to by Amanda Crowley. *"Poor Batty only trying to play with the ducks and you come along —"*

"Billy probably told him to do it," was Carrie's answer.
That had not gone down well at all with the aunt, who had
always considered herself a martyr first-class.

Carrie loathed this tall, slim, buckled-down woman. She
always seemed to be wearing riding gear of some sort. Tight
pants, tight boots, that day a jacket closed with metal clasps.
She had a mouth like a clamp that barely opened when she
spoke in angry little spasms. Her hair was metal-gray, but
fashionably done, pulled back in a fancy chignon from a
round face, slightly jaundiced from too much passing about
of the hunt cup, probably. It reminded Carrie of a poached
egg. Amanda Crowley considered herself very county, loved
to hunt and shoot, and was rumored to have her eye on Sebastian Grimsdale.

A wonderful pair, Carrie had thought, listening to the
spasmodic voice of Miss Crowley. The two of them might
mistake the rustles they made in the woods and shoot each
other.

"The Baroness will have to be told." The Baroness was
often approached by certain of the villagers who did not appreciate Carrie Fleet's ministry. It was always with that *you
must be told* excuse, though no one apparently ever thought
Amanda Crowley "must be told" about her own two.

This going to the Baroness always made Carrie laugh inwardly. The Baroness sometimes would, and sometimes
wouldn't, invite the complainants in. When she allowed

them an audience, it was in her withdrawing room, where she promptly withdrew her attention.

Thus while Amanda or Mr. Geeson or whoever happened to be that day's visitor was issuing an ultimatum, the mind of the Baroness was far away, strolling through an avenue of limes and plum trees, ripe fruit fallen underfoot, sunshade twirling slowly, milky hand lying on the arm of the Baron. That, or the faraway look had something to do with the gin in her teacup.

Carrie enjoyed imagining the Baroness's imaginings. Perhaps she embellished upon them in her own mind, she didn't know. But she had seen so many old photographs of what "La Notre" had once been — its summer house, its Grecian columns, its grounds and gardens completely out of place in Ashdown Dean.

There were times when Carrie's own arm replaced the Baron's as she accompanied the Baroness on her rambles through gardens long gone to seed or strangled with vines and grounds gone to moss and trees lichen-drowned. But the Baroness seemed to see in this adumbration of some garden Armageddon a mere need for the gardener to "see to" a few things. The cold stalks of dahlias she aimed her walking stick at and told Carrie to tell Randolph to see to them. Randolph was in his dotage and saw to nothing. Occasionally, Carrie had observed him leaning on a rake or a hoe and performing about as effectively as the crumbling statue at his back. Randolph also had a faraway look, but this was directed to the turf accountant's in the market-town of Selby. He would roll out his rickety bicycle and wobble off down the long drive, headed for Selby.

Given the Baroness's predilection to absent herself mentally from the felicity of the Crowleys of this world, it was left to Carrie herself to sit there and accept the hard coin of their complaints, like a parishioner passing the collection plate, as she literally passed the cake plate. And all the while marveling that none of the Ashdown Dean crowd had twigged it: the Baroness Regina de la Notre was either in a waking dream or dead drunk.

Although, of course, when she held her salons, Regina came up for air out of the past to join the present.

These were Carrie's reflections as she looked blindly across the bright water at the Church of St. Mary's and All Saints. The ducks, everlastingly hopeful, had been joined by two swans. She had the money for the Baroness's gin in her shoe, and would buy a half-loaf and come back.

Carrie started toward the sub-post-office stores, her mind again on the lady and man at Gun Lodge.

She allowed herself the vain thought that she didn't know which pair of eyes, deep violet or glittering green, she would have given her soul for. She had always hated her eyes, faded like her denim dress, hated her hair, her pale face — all of her. It was shameful, perhaps, in a world full of suffering, to want to be pretty. Carrie wanted to be absolutely smashingly beautiful. That was worse.

As she neared the store, she thought, well, at least she could buy bread, and that was more than a lot could do.

Ten

ry as she might, and huge as were the grounds of "La Notre," it seemed impossible for Carrie Fleet to circumvent the Baroness Regina. At eleven-thirty, the Baroness should have been taking her late coffee and brioche on the vine-tangled terrace overlooking the duck pond.

The Baroness was as unpredictable as her history. Her maiden name was Scroop, a Liverpudlian. The Baron Reginald de la Notre had made himself a fortune in fine leather gloves and it was indeed behind a glove counter in Liverpool that he had discovered Gigi Scroop. And had been bewitched (according to the Baroness) by her hands. Carrie had often been treated to the look of her graceful, beringed fingers when pouring another tot of gin or lighting another cigarette.

It wouldn't surprise Carrie at all if they'd married because of their names — Regina and Reginald — so they could call each other Reggie. "Gigi" had been the diminutive in Regina Scroop's family. Carrie wondered how she had got the Liverpool accent out of her speech. She even knew French; or enough of it to make people believe she even knew French.

"La Notre." What a stupid name in an English village,

Carrie thought, as she walked through the deer park, one part of her mind checking for signs of poachers. (The only person allowed to carry a rifle on the grounds was Carrie, an allowance made to herself by herself.) Before the Baron had got his chubby fingers on the property, the old house had been called "The Grange." The Baron (dead these fifteen years) had seen (according to the Baroness) the incredible possibilities of both house and grounds — the "estate" through whose history she had boringly sifted so many times that Carrie wondered there could be any more grains left on the mental beach. The Baron was a descendant of that famous gardener who had done Versailles. Carrie had been treated to enough pictures of famous gardens to make her feel like going out straightaway and trampling the lobelias.

Yet, she was sometimes sorry the Baron had passed on to his long line of flowery ancestors, for it would have been a lark to find someone else both as silly and determined as was the Baroness. To watch them take walks together, probably arm in arm, up and down the paths, past the Roman statuary, round the pools and ponds. What a team they must have been. She could not understand how anyone could have taken the simple *before* picture of "The Grange" and turned it into this enormous, ugly building of dark gray stone, bay windows bulging inappropriately underneath the battlements, a building that sat on a swell of ground overlooking the pretty green of Ashdown Dean, like a king of the toads on a lily pad.

Carrie walked in the covering shade of willows and immense dahlias, screened from the terrace, when suddenly a sun-hat popped up amongst the begonias and larkspur and asked her where she'd been.

Carrie answered with her own question. "What're you doing out here *gardening?*" making it clear that no occupation of Carrie's could match in idiocy the Baroness's being caught with shears in her ringed fingers.

"One must have an occasional bout with exercise." She

made it sound like flu. "Gillian didn't do the flowers *again*."
Snip. "You haven't answered. What've you been up to? Here,
take these, will you?" She handed Carrie a rough-cut bunch
of wilting lupines.

"You always think I'm 'up to' something."

"You always are. What's in that box? Oh, God, don't tell
me." The sun-hat disappeared, reappeared, a few roses
browned at the edges like burnt toast in her hands.

"A stray. I found it in the woods."

Beneath the sunshade of her giant hat, Regina squinted. "I
think you call them like spirits from the vasty deep." Her
shears stopped, midair. "That could be poetry. Did I invent
it? How wonderful."

Although Carrie had quickly put it down so the Baroness
wouldn't notice, the kitten was mewling. To divert attention,
she said, "You want me to get you some fags in the village?"

"Don't use guttersnipe words like that. It's moving."

"What is?"

"You know what. Oh, never *mind*." One of the cigarettes
she ordinarily plugged into her ivory holder was dangling
from the corner of her brightly painted mouth. The Baroness
pulled some money from her coverall pocket. When she
dressed for something, she dressed for it, and always, for some
undisclosed reason, carried money. The diamond earrings
seemed a bit out of place, however. "Did you bring the Tan-
queray?"

Carrie nodded. "But there was a fight with Ida. Over me
being too young to buy it."

"So what? You always win."

¤

The first thing Carrie Fleet had seen of the Baroness Regina de la Notre two years ago was a silver-buckled shoe on a
sheer-white-stockinged leg, followed by a mauve and gray-
blue dress, and then a matching hat. This mannequinlike dis-

play had descended from a cab outside of the London Silver Vaults. The face above the dress, however, was running on a different time schedule from the shoes, dress, and hat. It was painted and powdered to erase the difference, a good twenty years of it. The Baroness had (as for two years she had been advising Carrie to do) "taken care of herself." Avoidance of sunlight was important, she was always saying. A similar avoidance of gin and cigarettes might have had the same effect, allowing the sixty-year-old face to run neck-and-neck with the forty-year-old body.

As the woman disengaged herself from cab and cabbie, Carrie was further intrigued by her having a Bedlington terrier on a rhinestone studded lead — mauve, like the dress. And since the Bedlington was grayish-blue, it blended perfectly: a dog chosen to complement the ensemble.

Carrie, seated on her portable canvas stool, had already taken on a whippet and a poodle. Round her neck was a plastic-covered card. "You can't take the dog inside, madam."

The formidable woman stared. "Who are you?"

"I mind animals." The brief blaze of the look Carrie Fleet shot Regina de la Notre could have melted the glove leather shoes on her feet. "For a pound an hour."

The Baroness looked the situation over. The Alsatian was having a nap in a pool of sunlight. The poodle was doing the same beneath the canvas stool the girl sat on. Neither seemed to care that its owner had gone. Nor would, apparently, the Bedlington terrier, straining at the lead when the girl held her hand toward it.

Probably a witch, thought the Baroness. Covens of them all over England. "I find this amazing and, surely, illegal."

"Here's a constable coming. You can ask him."

Strolling slowly, hands behind him, seeming to enjoy the unearthly spring sunlight, the policeman looked as if he too might just curl up on the sidewalk and nap. The Baroness looked from him to the girl. "Kickbacks, probably. I suppose you want your money in advance. Or do you just hold the animals for ransom?"

"No, madam," said the unflappable girl. "Like I said, pound an hour."

As if to turn her words to gold, a handsome couple walked up the steps from the vaults and collected their whippet. The gentleman plucked two pound notes from his money clip. The girl took them and opened her little purse and returned fifty pence.

He seemed embarrassed. "Oh, heavens, my dear child —"

There was a look that the Baroness rather liked on the face of the dear child. It reminded her of the flower girl being taught to speak properly.

"You were only gone for just over an hour." She handed him the lead to his whippet. The dog seemed nervous and baffled; its sleep had been disturbed and, worse, it was to go back to the same old routine, the same old people, to be hauled about like a dog. It gave its temporary keeper a beseeching look. The girl returned the look, but let it go, like the realist she was.

The Bedlington was clearly ready to take the other dog's place in the sun.

Regina's tobacco-brown eyes followed the couple and the dog. "Part of the setup?"

Carrie Fleet flicked her a smile like someone tossing pennies. "If I may say so, madam —"

"You may not. Very well. Here's Tabitha, and you needn't wince. It's as good a name as any."

Tabitha lay down at Carrie's feet and the Baroness started down the steps. Then she turned, curious. "What were you going to say, anyway?"

"You don't seem to trust people much."

"Aren't you clever. I don't."

"Neither do I," said Carrie Fleet in a tone like dry ice.

There was forged between them an immediate bond. Mutual curiosity and reciprocal distrust.

She was the first interesting thing that had happened to the Baroness since the Baron had died.

Eleven

The negotiation for the life of Carrie Fleet was carried out in a run-down street near the East India Docks, but not in that dockside area lately running toward chic, where warehouses and crumbling waterfront properties were being bought up by the sorts of people who usually lived in mews in Kensington or Chelsea and realized that proximity to Harrods no longer did much for status. Decorators were followed by artists, actors, and retired brigadiers.

Although the general ambience of the Crutchley Street house had a certain warehouse flavor — orange crates doing service as tables — the Brindles, Joe and Flossie, weren't fortunate enough to have one of those properties the moneyed were looking for. It was one of several on this mean little street, where doorjambs and window moldings had been tarted up by Pakistanis and Indians with more of a flair for color — especially marine blues and rusty reds — than had the Brindles. They had decided to let well enough alone, a decision which extended both to their property and themselves.

The Baroness was sitting on an orange crate covered with an India-patterned spread and drinking tea the color of coffee from a permanently stained mug.

The cab at the door, from which the Baroness and Carrie had exited, had been regarded through the windows by several pairs of eyes. Probably, the last cab at the door in this street had been a hansom.

"Now, then," said Joe Brindle, the vest undulating over his loosened belt, "you're sayin' you was thinkin' a findin' a bit a work for our Carrie here?" He gave Carrie a friendly smack across the buttocks that made the Baroness, well traveled and used to the various breeding practices of many countries, somewhat uncomfortable.

Flossie, drinking a bottle of Bass, one thin leg tucked under her other on the sprung couch, said (for the dozenth time) "Well, I never." She kept curling and recurling a ringlet around her index finger. "Whatever'd you want t'do that for?"

The question that the Baroness had wanted to ask ever since she'd put her silver-buckled shoe out of the cab was: Whatever had *they* been thinking of when they took the girl in in the first place? Mercy and succor did not seem to be the Brindles' strong points. Sex and avarice would have beat them out by several lengths.

Then there were the others — children, dogs, cats — the last two categories fallen apparently into the hands of Carrie, and the Baroness hoped they knew how lucky they were. The dog Bingo, a rat terrier missing half a leg, had yipped and yapped and got up in a strange dance on its good legs like a circus animal the minute Carrie came into the house. It was the sort of animal that made the Baroness shudder — but then she had no interest in animals, anyway. Even the Bedlington did not belong to her, but to a friend in Eaton Place. She had thought it rather chic. The other dogs and cats could have been regulars or casuals; it was hard to say. A couple of them were growling over a dirty bone. That got them a boot in the side from Brindle. A one-eared cat got the same when it wound too close to his whiskey glass.

There was a young girl dozing under a pile of old blankets on another sofa, its springs coming through as on the one on which Flossie Brindle sat, a matched set. The girl was perhaps three or four years older than Carrie and hadn't moved at all except to wave a buzzing fly away and wipe her nose.

"Well, Joe, I'll be a monkey's." And she took another swig of Bass Ale and rewound the curl. "I knew we done the right thing when we found her."

Carrie might have been an investment in stocks.

"So where'd you say you lived, then?"

"Hampshire," said the Baroness crisply, only wanting to pay them off and be gone.

He scratched a closely shaven head, tugged at his ear. "Hampshire. Near that place — what's it called, Floss? Stonehenge, that's it."

"Stonehenge is in Wiltshire. The Salisbury Plain. I live in a village near the New Forest."

"New Forest. That's where you live?"

"Not *in* it, no. I would find that rather discommodious. The New Forest is more room than I need." She sipped the strange fluid and over the rim of the mug saw Carrie's mouth flutter in a tiny smile that quickly died. It made the Baroness think of a butterfly with broken wings.

Brindle blinked and then laughed. "Hear that, Floss?" he boomed, as if Floss were stone deaf. "More room — that's a good one. Okay. So you want Carrie here to come work for you. That it in a nutshell?"

"In a nutshell, Mr. Brindle."

"Well, I'll be a monkey's," said Flossie. "Imagine. Us findin' her wanderin' in the woods round Hampstead Heath, and here was you lookin' for her all this time."

It was the story the Baroness had given out, that Carrie was her younger sister's third cousin. "It's a small world," said the Baroness, taking out her silver cigarette case (which she watched them appreciate) while Carrie stood there, saying nothing, contradicting nothing.

Watching, thought Regina de la Notre, the world go by. Regina could have told the Brindles that Carrie was sister to Prince Rudolf of Ruritania and Floss would still simply have been a monkey's.

Of course, the richer the bird, the harder the fall when the Brindles brought it down with buckshot.

"That makes us some kind of relations-in-law." Joe winked.

"No, I don't think so."

He slid down in his chair, squinted up at the ceiling as if the price of one Carrie Fleet were printed in its spidery cracks, and said, "A course, Carrie puts bread on the table. Good girl, is Carrie. What'd you make today, luv?"

"Six pound. Pounds," she corrected herself. The Baroness Regina had noticed that Carrie Fleet's accent bore no resemblance to either of the Brindles', one East End, the other vaguely Northern.

"Jesus, you do better than them down t'the Sailor's Mate," said Flossie, swigging her ale.

The Baroness did not stroll her imagination down to the Sailor's Mate, where she imagined Flossie strolled often enough.

"It will also be one less loaf," she reminded Joe and Flossie.

He looked puzzled. "What's't?"

"Mouth to feed, Mr. Brindle."

Flossie stopped curling her hennaed locks and looked a bit sharper at the Baroness. "You don't mean you'd just take the girl away without no renumeration." She leaned forward. "Listen, we been seein' to Carrie here for five year, *five.*"

The United Kingdom had been seeing to Carrie Fleet. It

was obvious they were all on the dole. The giant color television and video machine would have attested to that. Extra
money for the poor little orphaned girl.

"Remuneration, of course. I shouldn't think of taking away
your chief means of livelihood."

Brindle had his eye so hard on his mark that he didn't even
get the insult. "How much were you thinkin', then? Not, a
course, we'd want to lose Carrie. Means a lot to us, Carrie
does."

"A thousand pounds perhaps?"

He pretended to think it over. Looked at Flossie, whose
finger was frozen in midcurl. Slapped the arm of his horsehair
chair and said "Done!" Then quickly added, unspilt tears
choking him, "Meanin' if it's okay with you, Carrie. She
could give you lots more than we ever could."

Carrie looked around at all of them and when she spoke,
her breath might have frosted the April air. "Maybe."

The Baroness was ambivalent in her feelings toward that
reply.

҂

The Brindles wasted no time the next morning in handing
over Carrie Fleet. Flossie's hand was busy with a wadded
hanky at her eyes, but since that took only the one hand, she
had one left over for her can of Bass Ale.

Joleen, the girl who had been snoring on the couch the day
before, appeared either sad or simply cross to see Carrie
leaving. The other children — stairsteps of two, three, and
four — did not appear to comprehend the solemnity of the
affair and were chalking graffiti on the sidewalk.

Only the animals seemed upset. Carrie said good-bye to
each one.

Breaking her vows of silence, Carrie remarked as they
drove across Waterloo Bridge, "You could've got me for

less." There wasn't a touch of pathos in her voice. Or humor, either. It was simply matter-of-fact.

The Baroness twirled a cigarette into a carved-ivory holder. "No doubt. A case of whiskey and several of Bass would probably have done it." She glanced at the shiny, battered hatbox Carrie was holding on her lap. There were airholes stuck in it. It seemed quiet enough. "A three-legged cur wasn't part of the bargain, however."

"You wouldn't want me to leave Bingo behind?"

"Yes."

"In case you're interested." Carrie stopped there, as if it were the end of a lengthy exegesis.

The Baroness waited. Nothing further was forthcoming. "Well? Interested in *what*, my dear girl?"

"Why Bingo's only got three legs. Wasn't born that way."

"I had inferred as much. Hit by a car, or something?" She tapped ash out the window. Frankly, she wished the rest of him had gone the way of the fourth leg.

They had spanned Waterloo Bridge, and she was thinking nostalgically of the old one, and poor Vivien Leigh standing in the fog. Or was it poor Robert Taylor? Both, probably. . . .

They were in Southwark, now, on the other side of the Thames and headed for Waterloo Station.

Carrie drew her companion's attention to a skirmish outside a dilapidated building, where several boys were throwing stones at a couple of mongrel dogs that had been searching for their breakfast in an overturned dustbin. "I found Bingo in an alley, round back of the docks. One of his legs was practically chewed off. That's the way it looked, anyway."

"How revolting. Don't bother with the details."

The details were forthcoming. "It wasn't chewed. Somebody'd beat it with a spanner. Or something like." Carrie's face was turned around, watching, while the cab was stopped at a light.

And then she looked at the Baroness. "I don't suppose you want to go back?"

"Back?"

Carrie hitched her thumb over her shoulder. Her expression was as hard as the stone that hit the dog. "There."

"I most certainly do *not.*"

The girl was rather alarming. But she said nothing else, just sat staring straight ahead. The Baroness took in her profile. It was, actually, quite good. Straight nose, high cheekbones. Magnificent pale blond hair. "Once we get you in some decent clothes," she said, enjoying her morning cigarette and hoping the train had a *real* dining car, "and scrubbed up, you'll be quite presentable."

"I'm not a potato," said Carrie Fleet.

The Baroness chose to ignore this. "You're not going to get that animal in a first-class car, you know. He'll have to go third."

Carrie Fleet was still looking back over her shoulder. Then she turned around. "You could just buy up all the seats in the car. Then there wouldn't be no — *any* —" she'd squinted her eyes like a person with a stammer "— bother from people."

"Good God! You *are* the most stubborn person I know."

"Second most," said Carrie Fleet, with her butterfly smile.

Twelve

The whitewashed cottages of Ashdown Dean straggled off like roses on a trellis, up the hill-rise of the High Street and down the other side, with winding roads as narrow as stems branching off, one of which was Aunt Nancy's Lane, where Una Quick had lately lived.

The bizarre incident of the death in the call box explained, Ashdown was returning to its daily rounds, with Ida Dotrice filling in at the post-office stores. Thus Jury knew that Constable Pasco was merely indulging the superintendent's whim. If he wanted to waste his time in the overcrowded cottage of an elderly woman, Pasco didn't care.

Pasco was leaning against the cluttered mantelpiece, chewing gum, as Jury stood with his hands in his pockets and looked around. "Certainly liked knickknacks, didn't she?" Pasco apparently felt the answer to this quite obvious, given the bits of shells, little stuffed birds, blown-glass animals, Presents from Brighton, the Isle of Man, and Torquay, their greetings written in flaking gold script across shaving mugs, gilt-edged cups and saucers. The little parlor was stuffed with memorabilia. "No family?"

"None I ever heard of," said Pasco, lazily chewing his gum.

Jury smiled. The constable's duties in Ashdown Dean were probably limited to stopping motorists going over the thirty-mile limit and checking locks at night.

"Why am I mucking about here, you're probably wondering." Jury was looking at a silver-framed photograph. A group in bathing costume, arms round one another, laughing by the seaside.

Pasco smiled sleepily. "True. But if you want to, I guess you have a reason."

Jury replaced the photo, sat down and lit a cigarette. He tossed the pack to Pasco, who took one and tossed it back. The constable, Jury thought, under that lethargic manner was nobody's fool. Maybe lazy or simply bored, but when he wasn't doing his sleepy act, you could see the blue eyes were very sharp.

"Did you think there was anything strange about Una Quick's death?"

The eyes opened; Pasco paused in the act of bringing cigarette to mouth. "Strange how?"

"That storm last night. It took down a couple of power lines and apparently Miss Quick's phone service with it. No one else on the phone nearby? Ida Dotrice?"

Pasco shook his head. "Una couldn't really afford one —"

"Who can? Go on."

"— but she was so nutty about her heart that she had one put in. In case something happened. And to call Farnsworth."

"You said she reported to him religiously, as he told her to do, by calling his surgery every Tuesday. Dr. Farnsworth must be an extremely dedicated doctor, to do that."

Pasco smiled. "If Farnsworth is dedicated to his National Health list, I'm the Chief Constable."

"No money in it."

"But a lot in private patients. Still, according to Una, that's what he told her to do."

"But she *did* have a bad heart."

"Damned right. When her dog died . . . Pepper, its name was. Poisoned on some weed killer." Pasco threw the butt of his cigarette into the cold grate. "It nearly killed her."

"Where was it found?"

Pasco nodded in the direction of the rear door. "Potting shed. Claimed it was locked, but Una was pretty absent-minded."

Jury thought for a moment. "Ashdown Dean goes uphill and the one call box is at the top. Not a very steep incline, maybe. But a woman with a heart condition whose pet had just died —? The storm and the hill. Would you've done it, Constable? It's pretty ironic, isn't it? The very effort of calling your doctor kills you. And there was that comment Miss Praed made about the umbrella. Why wasn't one found in the call box?"

"That storm came up pretty suddenly. She must have left before."

"Then that's even stranger."

Pasco frowned.

"That means, given the time of death as Dr. Farnsworth puts it, Una Quick was in that call box for at least a half an hour."

The constable looked around the cottage, still frowning. "The storm took out the service at the vicarage and the post office. They're working now." Pasco moved to the other side of the room and lifted Una Quick's receiver.

"But hers isn't," said Jury.

Thirteen

"I didn't insist she should ring me, Superintendent," said Dr. Farnsworth as they sat in his surgery in Selby. "It was, if anything, the other way around." He rolled ash from a Cuban cigar that must have come from some secret stock; it hadn't come from the local tobacconist. Indeed, the doctor's surgery had not been decorated by the National Health. Not with a Matisse on the wall and a marble sculpture of a fish on a desk whose polished surface the fish could have swum across.

"You know," continued Farnsworth, "the way many cardiac patients are. Obsessive about their hearts. Phobic. Which adds to the problem. She did ring me on Tuesdays, that's true, but not at my insistence. And not last night."

"Then Una Quick was lying?"

Dr. Farnsworth leaned back in his leather swivel chair, another gift from a private-patient list that Jury imagined was extensive. After showing his warrant card to the secretary, whose receding chin seemed to pull in even farther, turtle-wise, Jury had told her he'd be happy to wait until the two patients present had seen the doctor. The one who had just left had been wearing silver fox. The two remaining wore fashionable suits that hadn't come off the rack. All three were women. And as Jury sat observing Dr. Farnsworth now, he guessed that most of his patients were women. Farnsworth was a trim sixty-plus who had had his arm around the shoulder of the middle-aged patient he had escorted to the door (no buzzers here, apparently), giving the shoulder a reassuring pat.

His manner with men — certainly with Jury — was somewhat more brisk, somewhat less unctuous, somewhat less full of direct eye-contact. Jury didn't put this down to his being a policeman. He bet that was Farnsworth's general manner with men. All of his women patients were probably in love with him.

"I merely meant that many patients do become obsessed with their illnesses and want to believe you've a particular interest in them."

Jury did not bother to point out that Una Quick's story about the telephone calls was much *too* particular to be explained in that way. But he dropped the point for the moment.

"Why is all of this so important, Superintendent? And why would Scotland Yard be interested? Do you question my diagnosis?"

Farnsworth's expression was like becalmed water, not a ripple crossed it. If he was at all worried about Jury's visit, he was doing a superb job of hiding it.

"It was a friend of mine who found her," said Jury.

"Ah. The lady at the call box." He shook his head. "Devil of a thing to happen to a visitor."

Jury smiled. "I suppose it'd be a terrible thing to happen to a local, too. Were you surprised, Doctor? Cardiac arrest apparently from climbing up that hill?"

Farnsworth continued to roll his cigar in his mouth as his glance strayed about the room, a room he obviously took some pride in. "Una could have gone at any time."

Although the doctor did not appear to resent Jury's questions, still he was doing precious little by way of answering. Jury approached the central problem in another way. "Miss Quick must certainly have had a lot of faith in your patience, then, to call you every week like clockwork. And after office hours."

"It's not much trouble answering a phone call, Superintendent," said the doctor, expansively. "Wouldn't you do the same in your line of work for someone who went in fear of her life?"

"Yes. I might even insist the person call."

Farnsworth stopped rolling both the cigar and the chair. "I have a feeling you don't believe me."

"Sorry. The only other person who'd know is dead."

The doctor frowned. "Good God, Mr. Jury. Why would I lie about something so innocent as having a patient telephone me?"

Depends how innocent it is, mate, thought Jury. But all he said was, "It's true that Una Quick would have more reason to embroider — self-aggrandizement, maybe. What sort of person was she?"

Dr. Farnsworth shrugged and shoved the ashtray into line with his gold pen set. "Ran the sub-post-office stores, lived alone. No relatives except a cousin or two in Essex or Sussex. Perfectly ordinary old woman with an old woman's complaints. No kind of person, especially."

It was that comment that rather encapsulated everything Jury disliked about Dr. Farnsworth.

✗

The same could not be said for Dr. Paul Fleming, the veterinarian, whom Jury called round to see next.

His offices were Spartan and his patients on a lower social scale than Farnsworth's. But at least their fur was their own.

Paul Fleming was scraping a mass of tartar from the teeth of a large black tom while he talked to Jury. "I only knew Una, really, in relation to her dog. I guess that's the way I know most of the villagers. Haven't been here all that long. It was a terrible thing, that — I mean the dog. I guess you've heard about the poisonings." Paul Fleming shook his head. The cat lay quiet, anesthetized and into another night as dark as the one he apparently had come out of. Fleming had found him, he said, on his doorstep, like a patient come to call.

Jury started to take out a packet of cigarettes and remembered where he was and put them back.

"Later," said Dr. Fleming. "When I'm through with him we can have a smoke and a drink. I feel like I could drink the whole flaming bottle." He lifted the cat from the porcelain table and put it in a cage. "Okay, mate, when you wake you'll be able to eat again."

Now they were sitting in Fleming's small, crowded parlor — books stacked about, magazines on veterinary science. They were passing the bottle back and forth, topping up their glasses.

"You work hard, Dr. Fleming."

"Paul. Yes. I'm also an administrator at the Rumford Laboratory about a mile outside of town."

"Animal experimentation, I think."

"I love the way you put it. Sound like a bloody member of the Animal Freedom Front. There's research and research. A lot of people don't understand that."

Jury wasn't sure he did himself.

Fleming went on. "I suppose people think they can save themselves. From cancer. From thalidomide. After all, what's the life of a baby compared with a dozen cats?"

Jury smiled. "Several hundred, more likely."

Fleming just looked at him.

Jury changed the subject. "There was Una's dog, and, I understand, a cat and the bicycle-shop owner's dog. How do you explain it?"

"Accidents, that's all. The Potter sisters are known to be a bit 'peculiar,' to say the least. Their cat died from a dose of aspirin."

"Aspirin?"

Fleming nodded. "I'd given them some pills for the cat's allergy. Flat, white. They were screaming at one another that the other one — Sissy is half-blind — gave the cat the wrong pills." He shrugged. "It would take more than one, though." Fleming looked doubtful. "So someone had to make the mistake several times."

"Let's suppose none of these deaths *were* accidents."

"Hard to suppose. But I guess I'd probably bet on those Crowley kids — though that'd be going a bit far even for them. And they'd have to gain access to the food." He shrugged. "They said the cat got fed on the back porch. Someone could have got at it, I suppose. Some animal-hater. Grimsdale, maybe."

"The one who owns Gun Lodge?"

Fleming nodded. "M.F.H. Real snob, worse because he hasn't got the cash to keep the place going without turning it into a B-and-B. He nearly went bonkers when he found old Saul Brown's dog turning up the rosebushes. Actually got out his gun." Paul Fleming leaned his head back against the worn leather and considered. "There really aren't that many possibles. Amanda Crowley — Billy and Batty's aunt — maybe. Loves horses but that's all. And she's phobic when it comes to cats. But that would be a point in her favor, wouldn't it? She'd be terrified to get near one. Must play bloody hell with her in Ashdown. There're so many of them. I remember Regina — the Baroness —" He turned to Jury. "Have you met her?"

Jury shook his head. "Haven't had much of a chance to meet anyone yet."

Paul Fleming laughed. "You're in for a treat if it's your plan to go about questioning people. Anyway, the Baroness de la Notre, as she calls herself, unaware of Amanda's phobia, had a couple of cats wandering about during one of her salons. Amanda started screeching and fell into Grimsdale's arms. Maybe it was just an act, at that. But how anyone could be attracted to him is beyond me." Fleming stopped in the act of refilling their glasses. "Of course, the same could be said of *her*.

"So if you haven't met Regina, you haven't met Carrie Fleet?"

"Haven't had the pleasure, no."

Paul Fleming burst out laughing.

fourteen

Neahle Meara had pulled the covers up over her face, body stiff and straight, pretending to be Dracula. It was difficult with the kitten rising and falling with every breath. It would be nice to be able to sink long fangs into Sally MacBride's neck. It was dark. Dawn was just breaking outside the dormer window nearly strangled in creepers, but no light filtered through the covers over Neahle. It was also cold. Sally made Neahle wonder if death really might come in bat-form and pick you up with its talons (Sally's were long and lacquered) and take you off.

But it would have to drop you in a wooden box. That's the way her father had been buried. She lay there and tried to think how it felt — but he couldn't have felt, could he? Being dead? It was four years ago, but she remembered the wake and the sitting up and the singing and drinking and found it very strange they were having a party when her da was dead. It's not a party, Neahle, her gran had explained, it's but the way we see your dear father is taken into Heaven. Her mother had died giving birth to her. Her da she had loved because he was always in such a good humor and telling her how pretty she was, how her eyes reminded him of the lakes of Killarney.

It was supposed to be such good luck for her to have this English uncle with his pub in Hampshire who was so happy to take her in. For he could offer her so much more. And get her out of Belfast. Neahle remembered Belfast vaguely as a place full of bright shops on the one hand, and broken glass and boarded-up houses on the other.

Uncle John had the Deer Leap, and things had been all right for a couple of years until he had gone up to London and come back with a new wife who did not like Neahle Meara at all. Neahle was there before Sally, sitting at John MacBride's hearth. How did Sally MacBride know that she hadn't also been first in his heart?

Neahle sighed. Uncle John had changed a lot since Sally had come on the scene. And under the covers when Neahle sighed, the kitten rose and fell. The kitten was very small and probably not interested in what coffins were like and slept on, darkened over by covers though it was. Carrie had found it just yesterday and said she'd keep it part of the time with the other animals. Meanwhile, she'd fixed up an old book bag with air-holes at the bottom so that Neahle could smuggle it into the Deer Leap and up to her room. Carrie had even brought over a supply of Kit-e-Kat that she'd put in the play-house. No one ever went down there except Neahle, and you couldn't see it from the house. It was a perfect place to play with the kitten.

Neahle was not permitted to have pets. Only the chickens and hens in the henhouse.

"How can you call chickens pets?" Neahle argued. "You can't take them to bed with you or play with them or anything."

It was Sally who had laid down that law. It was always *that'll be enough of that, miss.* And turning to John Mac-Bride, *Such sauce.*

"Maybe I could have a fish, or something."

"Well, now, love," said Uncle John. "I don't see anything wrong with that, do you, love?"

This *love* directed at one of the most unlovable things Neahle could imagine.

They had been sitting round the dinner table, a dinner that Neahle herself had cooked, wearing an apron that hung nearly to the floor. Even at nine she could cook rings around Sally MacBride (née Britt) because her gran had started teaching her when she was five. They were having fish, which was what made Neahle think of it.

Sally, who had large horselike teeth, was picking at them in a most unladylike way. "A fish is it? One of those goldfish in a bowl to stink up the place. No, thank you, miss."

Neahle went round the table collecting the plates. Washing-up was also her job. "I was thinking more of a shark," she said, and ran from the room, jangling the cutlery on the plates just to make Sally MacBride turn sharply in her chair and yell *"Brat."*

Now this morning there was the problem of feeding the kitten, so she must rise from her coffin and dare the daylight before Sally the Bat came round to whoosh at her door and tell her to get up and fix the breakfast.

Then Sally would go back to bed, leaving Neahle to make the porridge and eggs. And there was Maxine Torres, a sullen Gypsy-like maid, who came in around eight, and would tell the world if she caught Neahle. She worked for the Baroness, too, sometimes, but Neahle liked the Baroness because she was kind of crazy and let Carrie do all the things that Sally MacBride would never let Neahle do. Most places Neahle was not supposed to go, but that made no difference to her, since if she only went where she was supposed to, she'd have to sit in a chair or stand at the stove all the time. But Neahle's visits to "La Notre" were different, for Sally believed in currying favor with those who might be useful or who lent to Ashdown what she called "tone."

Neahle left the kitten under covers scooped up for air and slipped her feet into her felt slippers. Light streaked the small windowpanes and cast its skeleton-finger across the dark floor. On the wardrobe door was a mirror in which Neahle could see herself in her white nightgown and, squinting her eyes, could imagine herself sliding ghostlike down the hall, quiet as the grave.

✕

Melrose Plant awoke in the chilly dawn light and pulled the duvet up to his chin. It was too short and left his feet uncovered, and the room was both cold and stark, but his brief encounter with the proprietor of Gun Lodge was enough to convince him that taking rooms anywhere else would be preferable to the steely gaze of Grimsdale over his morning gruel.

Porridge and toast as cold and hard as shingles was Sebastian Grimsdale's interpretation of Full English Breakfast.

Melrose wondered if he would fare better at the Deer Leap and lay looking at his feet, deciding he didn't like them, and contemplating rashers of bacon and fresh eggs and fried bread. The dinner last night had been quite presentable. Good English fare. When he told the MacBrides to offer his compliments to the cook, the wife had found this worth giggling over. But, then, she found a great deal to giggle about, whishing her brandy glass.

He was getting hungrier every moment and wished they did early teas. He had generously offered to give up his room to Jury, but Jury had had no qualms about dealing with Mr. Grimsdale's porridge — to the speechless delight of Polly

Praed. Anyway, Jury and Wiggins needed two rooms, and Melrose very much doubted Sergeant Wiggins would live out the visit.

Melrose frowned and pulled the duvet down over his feet, having considered them long enough to know he didn't like them; no more did he like the proximity of Polly Praed to Superintendent Jury. The violet eyes that regarded Melrose as a fly on the wall were simply dazzling turned upon Jury. Jury, fortunately, was not bedazzled by Polly. He found her seeming inability to knit words into sentences whenever she was in his presence puzzling. Melrose had always wondered at Jury's lack of awareness at the effect he had on the female sex. He only wished it would rub off on him. Plant closed his eyes and pondered. Certainly, he was rich enough, probably intelligent enough, even good-looking enough. Had he not thrown the Earl of Caverness and Viscount Ardry out the back door of Ardry End, he would even be titled, and *more* than enough. He tried to punch the pillows up, but they were too thin. It had annoyed Polly Praed no end that he had given up his titles, because she hated the titled family in her village of Littlebourne and would have loved to refer to *my friend, the Earl of Caverness.* Again he pulled the covers up to his chin. Perhaps it was his feet. He sighed and yearned for tea.

The welcome he had received at the Deer Leap was considerably warmer than the one at Gun Lodge, since there hadn't really been one. Though Grimsdale would have loved to rent the room, he somehow made it clear he'd rather not have anyone actually in it.

Here, however, the proprietors were all warm welcome, especially Mrs. MacBride, to whom he might have been a sailor returned from the sea. Looking at her, and getting her London bearings (Earl's Court out of East End, perhaps), Melrose imagined she might have had some experience in welcoming returning sailors. Sally MacBride, though not ravishing, appeared willing to *be* ravished. Though a bit overblown, she was still a looker, if you liked the type. She offered Melrose and Jury double brandies, a tight skirt that looked welded above her knees, and the story of her life. Or at least up until the early twenties, when her husband, John, a mild-mannered publican, twenty years older than his new wife, must have decided that Mr. Plant was not Boswell and stopped her. But heartily laughing at her escapades and peccadilloes all the while.

What miscrossed stars had brought the two together Melrose could only imagine: Sally was getting a bit long in the tooth and John MacBride had a nice, cozy business — the only pub in a pleasant village. But he did not appear to be a man of great sexual appetite. The wife, with all that flaxen, waxen-sprayed hair and pouty red mouth, was certainly one a lot of men wouldn't have minded having a bite of.

As his mind turned to Una Quick's death, Melrose was aware of something moving along the corridor. He decided to investigate and rose and tied his dressing gown. Anything would be better than lying in an old brass bed six inches too short for him.

Nothing, he thought, would take the chill out of the air, until he saw through the crack in the door a small, white figure, arms outstretched, coming down the hall. Apparently, It had heard his door open, for It stopped dead. The arms dropped as the little girl turned and fled with a look of horror back down the hall. Melrose saw a coal-black kitten getting shoved inside the room to the right of his.

The girl in the white gown disappeared, too.

He stood in the doorway to his own room and thought about this little scenario. The world of childhood was a world he felt best left to children; generally speaking, he did not engage in conversation, unless forced to do so, with anyone under twenty, and certainly had never himself *initiated* a meeting with an eight- or nine-year-old (for at such did he put her age). But in this case, curiosity overcame tradition.

He passed the MacBrides' room, where the door was slightly ajar and a night-light burning. Sally had had terrors of closed places ever since being locked in a closet, and her husband had leaned over to Melrose and whispered, *Claustrophobia, I call it.* Melrose heard the snores of John MacBride. The next room was the one into which the child had disappeared. He tapped on it; the door was open a crack, as if she had expected him, with his hood and sickle, to come calling. Given the look on her face.

Her head bent to the kitten in her lap, its coat as shiny-black as her bobbed hair, she said, "Now, I suppose you'll tell."

"Tell? Not only do I not know *what* to tell, I do not know *whom* to tell it to. Consider yourself safe."

There was a moment's scrutiny — a penetrating appraisal of his face — from eyes of such a rich blue one was surprised to see tiny knives in there. Then she looked at the window and the panes growing smoky white and put the kitten from her lap. "Okay. Maxine's probably not here yet, so let's go."

The carpet slippers slapped past him and as he hesitated, she motioned impatiently with a tilt of her head that he was to follow. He wondered if they were both to glide, arms outstretched, down the hall to their crypt.

"Where?"

"To the kitchen," she whispered over her shoulder, putting a finger against her mouth.

The kitchen. Tea. He followed down the narrow back stair where he felt the rising damp almost like tendrils of fog.

"What are we doing here?" He looked to see if there was a kettle on the hob.

She was busy sticking her head in a large fridge — there were two of them in the pub's kitchen, in addition to a large freezer and a huge butcher's table in the center of the room.

The floor was stone and icy-cold. Now she was dragging out milk and bits of cheese and things that she stacked along her arm. "It's got to be fed. You can carry some of this."

"I see. But why were you walking along with your arms out?" Melrose extended his own, in imitation. "Were you sleepwalking? Or, I mean, pretending to?"

"No. Here." She handed him a knife and a small plate. "Cut up the cheese in little bits. Thank you." This was added as an afterthought and without so much as tossing a sweet smile in his direction.

"You had your arms out —" Melrose was determined.

Crossly, she said, "We've got to be quick about this or Maxine or somebody'll come in. Can't you cut the cheese faster? You haven't done it at all. I'm nearly finished with mine. Do you eat venison?" She was looking toward the big freezer. "I think it's awful to kill deer and eat them. You must be the guest." She did not stop for confirmation or even temper her speech long enough to be surprised that the Deer Leap's single guest was down here doing scullery duty around seven A.M.

"For my labors, I would appreciate a cup of tea," he said, cutting the cheese in bits.

"We don't have time. Can't you make those pieces littler?"

"We're not feeding a mouse; it's a cat," he said.

"It's only eight weeks old. I'll get the milk and you run down to the playhouse and get the Kit-e-Kat." Her head was buried in the fridge.

Run to the playhouse. That made as much sense as anything in this dawn patrol. "I do not feel like running to the playhouse —" How could such rich, almost navy blue eyes give him that look full of splintered glass? "Oh, for heaven's sake. I shall do it only if you put the kettle on." Must he wheedle this person? "And *where* is this 'playhouse'?"

She looked as if she could have wiped the floor with him,

but her slippers slapped on the stone as she got out the kettle. "Just down the walk behind those trees. And don't dawdle, please."

Dawdle? Outside in his dressing gown? "Just have the water boiling," he commanded.

The playhouse was just that: a tiny place where he expected to find the seven dwarfs. As he turned the knob on the door he was thinking of Snow White. Hadn't she had trouble with her bed, too?

It was dark and musty in the the little place, and his eye fell on the supply of Kit-e-Kat in the corner.

Unfortunately, it had to travel over the body of Sally Mac-Bride on its way.

Melrose needed no warning about dawdling on his way back up the path. The sprite had probably tired of waiting — he had spent perhaps thirty seconds assuring himself the woman was, indeed, dead — and the kettle was whistling its long, screeching note.

He shoved it off the burner and went for the telephone.

fifteen

There was so little room in the playhouse, they kept bumping into one another, or at least Wiggins and Pasco did. Jury managed to keep his own space clear. Pasco had called the Selby station. They would try to get hold of Farnsworth, the doctor they seldom needed to call in as a medical examiner. If not him, someone from the local hospital.

"Not a mark, except for the hands." Jury got up. "Leave it until the M.E. gets here." He shook his head, looking around the single, square room. Perhaps twelve by twelve, he figured. Tiny. The few scraps of furniture — rocking chair, small bed, lamp, table — were clearly leavings from the dustbin men or unwanted sticks from the pub.

"MacBride's little girl's place?" He saw a sack of catfood in the corner.

"Niece," said Pasco, still looking wonderingly at Melrose Plant, now wearing a Chesterfield coat over his dressing gown.

Plant was getting damned irritated. "Constable Pasco. I *wish* you'd stop looking at me that way."

"I just can't figure out what *you* were doing down here — getting a can of Kit-e-Kat, you said?" Pasco gave him a flinty smile.

"Hell," said Melrose.

"Stop it, both of you." Jury was not happy.

Neither was Plant. "Look, what I really wanted was *tea*. So I followed the ghostly child to the kitchen —"

"Neahle," said Pasco.

"What? What sort of name is that?"

Pasco, used to sleeping in until nine, yanked from bed before eight and with another death on his hands, was not happy either. "Neahle Meara. Irish."

"Nail? What an awful name for one so young."

"Spelled N-e-a-h-l-e."

"Oh. Rather pretty."

Jury had picked up an enamel doorknob, handkerchief wrapped around it. "Bag this, Wiggins."

Sergeant Wiggins had been standing hunched in the doorway. There wasn't room for a fourth. He took a plastic bag from a supply he carried about like cough drops. "Shouldn't we wait for the Selby —"

"Probably, but I'm afraid of too many more feet mucking up this place. We've probably done enough damage as it is."

Plant said, "Look, I didn't touch anything."

Jury smiled up at him from his examination of the metal stem from which the knob had come off. "I know that." He got up. His head nearly brushed the ceiling. "You only came for the Kit-e-Kat."

Pasco smiled. Melrose smiled back.

Pasco was kneeling where Jury had kneeled, looking at the inside of the wooden door. "Terrible. It looks like she was trying to claw her way out."

"Claustrophobic," said Plant, frowning. "You remember how she was talking about cracking their bedroom door at night." Plant bent to look at the marks. Splintered wood and blood.

Jury could tell from the state of the fingers where the streaks of dried blood on the door had come from. "Absolute panic." He frowned and turned to Pasco. "Why would she be down here, anyway, Pasco? How well did you know her?"

Although Pasco's *about as well as anyone else, I guess* was casual enough, Jury noticed the flush spreading upward from his open collar. "I don't know why she'd be down here."

After the Selby police pathologist had examined the body and it had been zipped up in a rubber sheet, he put the cause of death down to heart failure.

"Like Una Quick."

"Brought on by fright, from the looks of it," said the pathologist. "If she was, as you say, a claustrophobic."

Detective Inspector Russell, from the Selby C.I.D., shook his head. "I'll be damned." He looked at Jury unhappily, whether from having Scotland Yard here or from a second death in this tiny village, Jury couldn't say. "What the hell was the woman doing down here?"

"We don't know. Any objections to my being here? It was a friend of mine who discovered Una Quick's body."

Inspector Russell didn't seem to mind; indeed, he looked relieved. If Scotland Yard wanted Selby-Ashdown corpses, they could have them. "I'll check it with the Chief Constable. That door —" Again he shook his head. "Knob just came off?"

"Maybe."

Russell took out his handkerchief and tried to twist the stem. It was old and rusted and wouldn't give. "She couldn't get it back on." The iron fitting inside the porcelain was broken, making it impossible to fit the knob to the stem. It was a very old doorknob.

"Let's go talk to MacBride. Does he know?"

"I took the liberty," said Melrose, "of informing him there'd been an accident. In a word, yes. He knows."

"Would you mind if my sergeant went along?" asked Jury, who was looking around the tiny house, his gaze finally fixed on the chair and the lamp. "And Mr. Plant?"

"Your sergeant, yes. And Pasco." He squinted at Melrose Plant. "But I don't see why —"

"He found the body," said Jury.

"Okay. What about you?" A mild suggestion that Scotland Yard was leaving the dog's work to the Hampshire constabulary.

"I'd like to talk to the girl — what's her name?" he asked Pasco.

"Neahle Meara."

"Ask her to come down here." At Plant's look, Jury said, "No, I won't show her the inside of the door. I want to talk to her, away from the others."

Then Jury added, "And tell her to bring her kitten and a can opener." He grinned.

✕

She stood framed in the doorway, clutching a gray cloth coat around her and holding what looked like a schoolbag.

Jury was surprised by her black hair and deep blue eyes, now smudged underneath and looking scared. He hadn't seen her in the Deer Leap; although he knew she wasn't the daughter, he'd expected someone with MacBride's washed-out coloring. This little girl was definitely not washed out; she was beautiful.

"Hullo, Neahle," he said. "Is the kitten in the book bag?"

Wordlessly, she nodded and chewed her lip. Then she stepped over the sill and said, with as much defiance as she could muster, "You can't take him away. He didn't do anything."

"Good God, whatever made you think I'd want to do that? I just thought maybe you'd like to give him his breakfast."

"Lunch. He had some cheese for breakfast, and milk."

"Lunch, then." Jury smiled. They might have been here for no other reason than to confirm the kitten's eating habits. It poked its black head out of the bag and blinked.

Neahle pulled it all the way out and set in on the floor, but made no move toward the catfood. "I heard about Sally — Aunt Sally."

That she didn't want to call her "aunt" was clear. And that she wasn't sorry the MacBride woman was dead was equally clear.

That, unfortunately, meant guilt could fall on her perhaps suddenly like a brick, hard and fast.

She was sitting in a troll-sized chair, picking at the flaking blue paint, "It's too bad." She did not look at Jury because she couldn't work up the appropriate tears, he bet.

"Yes. I thought you could help."

She looked up, then, interested. "I've got the can opener." She said it as if the Kit-e-Kat might be by way of helping.

"Toss it here." She did. Jury pulled a can from the bag and opened it. Then he put it down for the kitten, who obviously had had its fill of cheese.

"Why do you carry — what's its name?"

"Sam."

Jury nodded toward the book bag. "That's got holes in it for air."

"I know. That's to smuggle it in and out of the house. Sally"— and she inclined her head again —"wouldn't let me have pets. Said they just dirtied the place up."

It sounded consistent with the little he'd seen of Mrs. Mac-Bride. "That was smart of you."

"Oh, *I* didn't think it up. It was Carrie. She's my best friend. She found the kitten in the woods and fixed the bag. It was yesterday."

It was almost as if the fact of the kitten, Sam, had brought about this tragedy. Now she was groping in the bag and brought out an apple. "Would you like this for your lunch?"

"Thank you," said Jury gravely, as she handed it over. It was the first bribe he'd ever taken. "I don't know Carrie. I've only heard her name. Is she a school chum, then?"

Neahle laughed and put her hand over her mouth, which she smoothed out as if she were smoothing out her coat. Laughter in the house of death was hardly right. "No. Carrie doesn't go to school. The Baroness's secretary teaches her, or something. She's lots older than me. Fifteen. I don't know why she likes me."

Best friends, like kittens and aunts, could disappear easily in this world, her worried look said.

"I can't imagine why she wouldn't. Age doesn't make any difference."

"How old are you, then?"

"Quite old," said Jury solemnly. Thinking of Fiona Clingmore, he smiled and added, "I'll never see forty again."

Her eyes widened. "You don't look *nearly* that old."

"Thank you. Listen, Neahle. You know your aunt — Mrs. MacBride — was found in here."

Solemnly, she nodded, watching Sam now batting a tiny ball of wool she'd tied to the lamp cord for him.

"Did you ever know her to come down here before?"

"No. No one comes here but me, and sometimes Carrie."

"Okay. When was the last time you were here?"

"Two days ago."

"Did you keep the door closed?"

She looked puzzled.

"I mean, was the knob missing from the inside of the door? Fallen off its iron stem?"

She frowned. "I suppose so. I didn't much notice." Neahle scratched her ear. "It was dark."

If there'd been wind, it could easily have banged the door

shut. "Would you have been scared if you'd got locked up in here?"

She seemed surprised. "Me? No. I like to come here and read and sometimes I go to sleep on the bed there." She was watching Sam the kitten, now clutching the wool and swinging like a metronome from the lamp cord. "You could scream if you got locked up in here, but it's so far from the house —" She stopped watching the kitten and put her head in her hands.

"There was a wind last night, too. Neahle, you can't love everyone you think you should. When they won't let you have pets, and have you do the cooking. Why should you?"

She looked up at him. Then down. "You didn't eat your apple."

"Did you ever know Sally to come here?"

Neahle shook her head. "Why would she? She didn't even want *me* to."

"Maybe she would to, say, meet a friend."

"Like men?" Neahle was trying to look worldly-wise.

Jury smiled. "Like men."

Neahle scratched her ear. "Well, there's that Mr. Donaldson. He's creepy. Carrie says so. He works at Gun Lodge."

"Anyone else?"

She chewed her lip and shook her head.

Wouldn't have mentioned Pasco, even if she'd known. Jury picked up her apple and rubbed it on his raincoat. Her look seemed to ask, Are you going to do something magical?

He crunched the apple, leaned back in the chair, and watched Sam swinging. Sam dropped from his perch and came over to sit and stare up at the new person.

Neahle started to cry.

"Not to worry, Neahle." Jury picked up Sam and put him in Neahle's lap, where its shiny black fur was wetted with her tears. Then he sat back and simply waited until the worst of it was over.

The end of the cord from which Sam had been swinging led up to a socket and a blue-shaded lamp. "You came down here a couple of days ago, you said. Did you come down at night?"

Neahle chewed her lip.

"I won't tell." He nodded at the books. "Did you read, then?"

"Of course." She nodded to a little stack of books. "*Sam Pig*, that's my favorite. I named Sam after him. I suppose you can name a kitten after a pig." She seemed doubtful. "Anyway, I sneaked out of bed."

Jury turned his head on the back of the rocker. "What happened to the light bulb, then, do you think?"

x

None of them, particularly John MacBride, had been sitting very comfortably in the bar during the questioning of the husband.

Wiggins pinched the bridge of his nose and said, "Going up to London, was she? For how long, Mr. MacBride?"

"Few days. To visit a cousin."

Wiggins wrote down the name of a Mary Leavy who lived, said MacBride vaguely, "Somewhere in Earl's Court."

Melrose could have constructed any number of scenarios, taken from all of those mysteries he'd suffered through for the sake of Polly Praed. It was such a cliché. Wife going off to London, then mysteriously "disappearing." Fun for Crippen and Cream. But not, it would seem for MacBride, who seemed to be crumbling like the huge log sparking and splitting in the fireplace.

Detective Inspector Russell's smile was tiny. Melrose could almost read his mind. It's always the family. Dead wife, find the husband.

"And how was she to get there?" asked Pasco.

"How?" MacBride's eyes were glazed when he pulled his head from his hands.

"Yes. You said she was going to London, John."

"Oh. Train from Selby this morning."

Pasco prodded him gently. "But to Selby?"

MacBride wiped his hands over his thin hair. "Someone at the Lodge going to drive her. Donaldson, I think."

How nice, thought Melrose.

"Mrs. MacBride suffered from claustrophobia, I believe," said Russell.

MacBride nodded. A shadow like a raven's wing passed over his face as if the thought of Sally's being trapped in that house were too much for him.

"I'd have thought," said Russell, "when that door closed and she couldn't — well, let's leave it for the moment." He must have seen the look on MacBride's face, too.

Pasco put it in a more roundabout fashion. "You can't see the playhouse from the pub, not with that screen of trees. And I expect you can't hear — it's a bit far, there by the river."

MacBride only nodded.

Melrose put in: "There was a howler of a wind last night, too."

Wiggins couldn't have agreed more, but Russell was looking at Plant as if he couldn't imagine this guest in the Deer Leap offering anything of substance. The testimony of someone who would wander out to a playhouse at seven in the morning to get catfood . . .

"Splintered wood," said Russell, "long marks as if she'd tried to —" Again, some more humane instinct took over.

"Sorry, John," said Pasco. Light filtering through the fussy chintz curtains scooped out hollows in MacBride's cheeks. "Maybe you should lie down, John. We can talk to you later."

"Where's Neahle?" asked MacBride, looking a bit wildly around.

"Asleep," said Wiggins, snapping shut his notebook.

Wiggins might have had more sense than all of them.

Sirteen

$\mathfrak{J}$ury wondered when the driveway would end and who had managed, in what couldn't have been more than an eighth of a mile, to devise the tortured approach to "La Notre" that in its twists and turns must have been like a Disneyland adventure-game. He expected something to jump out at every turn.

And at that moment in his thoughts, he had to veer and brake, barely missing an old man on a bike careening around one of the curves and not seeming bothered at all about scrapes with death. Must belong to the place, must be used to it, thought Jury, starting up again.

The surprise-package at the end of his deadly drive through deep rainpools and littered branches was a huge house whose towers he had seen from the Ashdown Dean road not far below. It was architectural gimcrackery at its worst. Where the original house left off was clear. It had played its part innocently enough as an old manor house or a draughty vicarage. Its design was pleasant and traditional, mullioned panes set in slabs of gray stone, ivy-bound. But to this house had been added towers, oriel windows, and cathedral windows, these last with a topping of painted bargeboards, like icing on a cake, utterly out of keeping with anything else. English, Italian, medieval, ecclesiastical all jousted for first place.

To round it off, from what he could see when he got out of his Vauxhall, there must have been a large expanse of Italianate garden behind the house. Jury just glimpsed a statue, a pagodalike bridge, a Corinthian column in the far distance.

None of this marvel, which made him want to laugh despite the reason for his visit, had been seen to — neither house nor grounds — in what must have been years. The ivy crept, the stones crumbled, the branches fell. Round those mullioned panes were cracks that must have let all the weather in Ashdown Dean come to settle here at "La Notre."

His card was taken on a plate of tarnished silver by a waiting maid in a cockeyed cap, hastily pinned on for the occasion.

While Jury waited for an audience with the Baroness, he looked around the commodious entryway. Here England, Greece, and Italy competed. Between beams of dark wood, Grecian-like columns held sculpted heads (that reminded him unpleasantly of those once stuck up on Traitors' Gate). The ceiling moldings were graced with cupids and garlands. The floor was green marble, the wide staircase mahogany. "La Notre" made up in money for what it lacked in taste.

Jury was admitted to an enormous room to his right, out of keeping with the hall, all breezy and bright, a sort of solarium, with plants everywhere. On the walls left and right, two identical *trompe l'oeil* murals. They seemed to be a reflection not only of each other, but of the real scene between them — on either side of a marble fireplace, french doors led to separate stone paths that in turn led to the wide gardens beyond. Jury blinked. It was worse than seeing double.

"Fools you, doesn't it?" said the woman on the green chaise of watered silk.

Her smile was as tricky as the mirror-image of the murals. Jury returned the smile. "You're the Baroness Regina de la Notre?"

"No. I'm her double. Two of everything. Good idea?"

"Maybe. Only one of me, though."

"Pity," she said, looking him up and down. Then her eye drifted to the card she held. "A superintendent, no less." Waving the hand that held the card, she invited him to sit.

Her dress was not his idea of eleven in the morning, magenta with a sprinkle of sequins, a violent shade that matched her lipstick and rouged cheeks. The bones were high and aristocratic.

From her velvet chaise (in keeping with herself, but not the plant-gorged room) she said, "A Scotland Yard superintendent. I'm impressed."

That it took one hell of a lot to impress the Baroness was quite clear from her tone.

She seemed as much a part of her surroundings as had the tricky driveway, the crumbling walls, the deceptive vista of the *trompe l'oeil* murals. Her smile was slightly unpleasant, not the result of ill will, but of dull teeth. Too many cigarettes, and, he supposed, catching a whiff as he had shaken her hand, too much gin. As she looked at the wall behind him, she said, "The Baron — my late husband — was fond of that particular school of French painting."

And, thought Jury, the Italians, the British, the Greeks . . .

She leaned forward, offered him a cigarette from a pedestrian crumpled pack rather than the gold box. "It's Una Quick you've come about, I expect. Wasn't that heart of hers at all, was it? Murdered, wasn't she? Not surprising, is it? It's her Nosy Parker business with the post, isn't it . . . ?"

Jury cut into the barrage of questions. "Why do you think Una Quick was murdered?"

"Because you're here, obviously."

Again, Jury smiled. It was a smile unmarred by tobacco stains, cynicism, deviousness, or anything else that might make a witness or a suspect throw up a guard. It had the opposite effect: they let down the guard. "I came here because of a friend."

Regina de la Notre stopped being arch. She merely looked at him and said, "Perhaps, but I'm not the friend, so you're poking about for other reasons. Una Quick was a simpering little mouse of a woman who ran the post-office stores and had a right rave-up with other people's post —"

"You're suggesting she read the villagers' post?"

"No, I'm *assuring* you she did."

"How do you know?"

"Because I posted a letter to myself from London that I got someone else to write — as I'm quite sure Una knew my hand — and turned the second page upside down. When she read it, she quite naturally had to turn it and forgot to turn it back. Or, even if some part of her little sewer of a mind took note, it discarded the notion that such a small thing might be important."

"That's very interesting. A different impression of Miss Quick than I'd got so far."

"Only because most of the people in Ashdown are idiots. Tea?"

She raised a silver pot, which had to be cold by now. Jury refused and she reached behind the chaise. "Gin?"

"Sounds better than tea." He smiled.

"I thought you'd think so." She poured some into a teacup. "Always knew that business about policemen not drinking on duty was bunk. How the hell would you get through a day of your line of work without it? Here."

Jury took the cup of gin from the beringed hand. He was

rather surprised. Though he wasn't going to drink a cup of gin, at least it had been offered with something like sympathy, something he doubted she plied to excess. The Baroness continued with her fund of information as she stuffed a cigarette into a long holder. Also sequined. "And now there's the MacBride woman."

The sip of gin Jury had taken burned his throat. "And just how did you know that? Her body was discovered only a couple of hours ago."

She raised her gin and eyebrows at the same time. "God. In a couple of hours the Ashdown Dean scandal could travel to Liverpool and back. My hometown. You probably noticed I am not French." Two possible murders did not seem of much more account than her Liverpudlian background. "Carrie Fleet told me."

"Carrie Fleet?"

"My charge. More or less. Neahle Meara came running up the drive an hour ago. She tells Carrie everything. Though I doubt she understands most of what she tells. I'm still debating whether MacBride was sleeping with our constable or that oily head keeper, Donaldson. Or both." She raised the pint of gin in invitation.

Jury shook his head. "Why don't you tell me what you know, then?"

Having poured herself another tot, she screwed the cap back on the bottle, and looked up at the ceiling through tendrils of smoke. "I'll try and condense it. Otherwise, you'll be stopping here all day. I told you about Una and the post. And that MacBride piece of fluff. If someone killed her, I'm quite sure it wasn't John. That, I believe, was true love, worse luck for him. I myself made a marriage of true love. No man since Reginald — the Baron — has interested me. Had you come along twenty years ago, things might have been different. Loaded with charm, aren't you?"

Jury smiled. "I only just got here."

"How tiresome." She sighed. "Charm, like a falling star, can be seen in a flash."

"Thanks. Continue."

"Well. Amanda Crowley is hot on the trail of Sebastian Grimsdale, though I imagine he'd rather sleep with a horse. I hope you do not think our Constable Pasco is stupid or lazy. That's all an act. Farnsworth, on the other hand, is both, which is not to say he's not capable of murdering the entire village. Paul Fleming, our veterinarian, is exceedingly clever, handsome, unmarried, and my secretary appears to be in love with him. Her name is Gillian Kendall. I expect you've heard the names of these people if you haven't already met them. As for myself, I prefer to keep behind the battlements here, in regal splendor, and let the others make asses of themselves. Occasionally, I invite some of the asses here. To what I call a salon. I don't really know what that means, but Grimsdale and la Crowley appear to think I am loaded —" quick smile "— I mean with money. And that allows me a certain ascendancy when they come to complain about Carrie. The local RSPCA. She turned the Baron's arbor into a sort of animal refuge. I am not fond of animals. That's where I found her. Outside the Silver Vaults —"

This enigmatic statement was cut short by Jury's looking up, suddenly, to see a girl and a woman appearing like dream figures at each of the french doors. Again, he thought he was seeing double: they might have been figures in the mural, each of them coming to a dead stop with her foot just over the sill when she saw Jury.

Regina turned her head and looked from one to the other as if they were party-crashers. "Oh, it's you. Gillian Kendall, Superintendent Jury."

The woman came in, holding out her hand. The other arm held some Michaelmas daisies. "How do you do?"

"Original as always, Gillian."

Gillian Kendall gave her employer a tiny smile. Used to her put-downs, probably. Jury couldn't help staring at her, though she was not a beauty. Except for the Grecian nose, her features were unexceptionable — mouth too wide, eyes narrow. But her hair and eyes were a lustrous brown — hair more of an auburn — and the very plainness of the prim gray dress with its high neck and long sleeves drew attention to the body underneath it. He wondered if she knew this. He watched her arranging the flowers, brown-tipped from frost, in a vase. No beauty, but the most sensual woman Jury had seen in a long time.

He turned to see the girl staring at him. But she hadn't moved from the frame of the french door at whose sill she stood, dead still.

"Oh, don't be such a stick, Carrie." Regina waved her impatiently into the room. "Carrie Fleet, Superintendent." She turned to Carrie Fleet. "Superintendent Jury is with Scotland Yard."

That announcement brought to Carrie's face no hint of surprise, pleasure, bewilderment. But she did come in. Not, Jury thought, because of the command; she might have come or gone as she chose. She did not offer her hand. Jury felt the air stir when she walked in, felt a subtle change in the atmosphere — a pause. Gillian had stopped in her act of arranging the poor bouquet; Regina drew her lap rug a bit more closely. And all the time she had kept pale blue eyes on Jury.

"Well, good lord, girl, at least say hello."

"Hello." That she said no more was not a deliberate slight. Perhaps this was the way she marshaled her forces, moving carefully from trench to trench, gaining a bit of ground here, another inch there. Jury wondered only what the battle was. She made the single movement of brushing her long hair back across a shoulder. It was platinum, the sort of blond hair that made one think it could turn, overnight, to pure silver. She was a marvel of self-control. Indeed, for those few moments she had controlled the room. Involuntarily, Jury looked at the clock to see if it had stopped.

After telling the Baroness she needed money for more chicken feed, she turned and left through the french door.

Regina topped up her gin-laced tea and said, "What a trial."

Gillian Kendall smiled slightly at the vase. "She's the only one you like, and you know it." Then she excused herself and left through the door to the foyer.

"God," said Regina, screwing a cigarette into her holder, "you can imagine how sprightly the conversation is round the dinner table."

"They both did seem rather shy." That was certainly not the word for Carrie Fleet.

Nor did Regina think so. "The girl has been called in to our local police station over half-a-dozen times."

"Why?"

"Because she *will* go wandering about the village seeing which cats and dogs are receiving what she considers adequate attention and which are in their death-throes. She did not care for the way Samuel Geeson kept his mongrel leashed in his backyard, and unleashed him and took him along to Paul Fleming and got him to call the RSPCA." Regina rolled the ash from her cigarette. "I found her in London. She had been living with a couple named Brindle. The Brindles had in turn found *her*, wandering in a wooded area of Hampstead Heath. Amnesia, they said. The Brindles knew where the dole money was. One thousand pounds I paid them, and they're putting the bite on me for more. Why on earth they think I'd be ripe for blackmail, I've no idea. Of course, I suppose they *could* claim I'd abducted her." Regina arched an eyebrow. "I really think *one* abduction is quite enough for one child, don't you?"

She reached round to a majolica jar and drew out a letter. "Here, have a look. Perhaps you can do something."

The two pages — a bit grimy and just edging toward literacy — took first a whining and then a honeyed tone. Jury said, "You didn't tell me she'd been given a bad blow to the head."

"Dear Superintendent, I did not know. I believe they are playing it for tears. Presumably, that accounts for the amnesia."

"It's a rather odd letter." Jury turned the pages over. Nothing on the back.

"I can assure you, the Brindles have their odd little ways."

". . . so we thought, taking enclosed into account, another five hundred might be worth your time. I remain, truly yours . . ." and a flourish of a signature. "What does he mean?"

Busy measuring out her gin, Regina just looked at Jury. "That he wants five hundred pounds, Superintendent. Even my spongy brain could ascertain that."

"Mind if I keep this?"

She waved the letter away. "By all means. Poor Carrie. Her name isn't even real. So there it is, she came to me with no documents at all."

"You make her sound like a purebred dog with dubious credentials."

She laughed. "Ah, Carrie would like nothing *better* than that comparison."

Jury smiled. "What about Gillian Kendall?"

"She's a Londoner and was having morning coffee in the local tea-palace when she overheard a conversation that I was looking for a secretary. I was beginning to bore myself, though that might be hard to believe, and when she came up the drive to offer her services six months ago I said yes on the spot. Couldn't stand to advertise and have half of Hampshire on the doorstep. But I'm not sure I care for her very much. I dislike people who walk on tiptoe and always seem to be carrying something in their hands — vases, decanters, flowers. Who knows but underneath there might not be a knife or a gun?"

Seventeen

Hard to believe that Gillian Kendall had a knife or a gun hidden under the cardigan she kept drawing more closely about her.

They were walking between the privet hedges that made up the maze, another of the Baron's practical jokes, she told him. "It's very carefully constructed," said Gillian Kendall.

"Isn't that the idea behind all mazes?" Jury thought Regina's assessment of Gillian Kendall was off the mark. She did not walk on tiptoe, nor did she seem nervous. On the contrary, she struck Jury as composed. Composition. It was the right word, if one were an artist. An extra brushstroke here and there would have colored over the too-pale cheek, brought a spark to the eye that would have doubled its effect.

"It's quite intricate," she went on. "For one thing, it's round. It can't help but give the impression a person is going in circles."

"Metaphorically speaking, a person usually is."

She stopped and looked at him. For a moment he thought she might be going to say something less oblique. But what she said was, "I've got lost here several times. The Baron apparently wanted to make sure that once his wife got in here, she couldn't get out. Oh, no malice. None. He liked games. This one I imagine would be sexual hanky-panky." Gillian looked away. "Funny. She speaks of him with surprising devotion. I would have thought she'd only have done it for the money."

"You don't care for her very much, I take it."

A gust of wind whipped her hair, even in this privet-sheltered place. Hiding the little row of buttons that marched up her prim dress by pulling the cardigan closer, she said, "I honestly don't know. She's like a wine that hasn't aged well." Gillian laughed. "A sixty-five Bordeaux, perhaps."

"A bad year?"

There was a pause as she picked at the hedge. "A very bad year."

Jury didn't think she was talking about wine.

Gillian looked along the curving path they had taken, one they could have continued along, or taken another to their right. "We've got three options," said Gillian. "Go on, go back, or go right. I leave it to you. Which way?"

There was an arched opening in the hedge. Through that he could see several others, like a series of archways down a long hall. It was much like the mural. "Well, that vista is a trick, I'd say. It appears so obviously an escape that it probably leads straight back to the center of the maze. So I'll take the fourth option."

"There are only three. Back, forward, out."

"There's also down." Jury enjoyed the feel of her arm as he pulled her to one of the benches they'd passed. "Strategically placed. Let's sit."

Shaking her head, she sat down. "Not fair."

"I disagree. Perhaps we can talk our way out. Or I can. After all, you know the way, and you've been leading."

The eyes she turned on him were cool. "You think I've deliberately led you into a trap?"

Jury smiled. "Sure."

"I don't understand. What have I said?"

"It's what you haven't. You've been having a hell of a good time walking round here, telling me about the Baron and his little practical jokes. But I would think that, knowing I'm from Scotland Yard, you'd wonder why I'm here."

"Why are you, then?"

"You must have known Una Quick."

She frowned. "Everyone did. But you're not here on her account —"

Jury interrupted. "A few days ago her dog was poisoned."

"That's right." She shivered and pulled her cardigan closer. "It was awful for Una. She was a sick woman, anyway. Paul — Dr. Fleming — he's the local vet . . ."

"I've met him. What about him?" Given the way she hesitated over the name, Jury wondered if the handsome Dr. Fleming was the reason for another bad year.

"Only that he said Una claimed the door to the potting shed was locked."

"Do you put that down to Miss Quick's forgetfulness? Or a local animal-hater?"

"That's hard to believe. But if I had to, I suppose I'd say it was the Crowley boys. They're awful. One truly is retarded, and the other acts as if he were. I can't think why Amanda doesn't put Bert — they call him 'Batty' — in an institution, instead of that 'special school' she sent him back to."

Looking through the corridor of openings, Jury said, "Institutions can be pretty grim places." He remembered his own years in the orphanage the social services had put him in after his mother had been killed in the last bombing of London. He had been six, but he would still, in his mind, walk the cold corridors, sit on the brown-blanketed bed, taste the watery potatoes. "Maybe she loves the boy too much."

"Amanda loves Amanda." Her profile, above the collar pulled up around her chin, was like the sculpted profile of one of the statues. "It allows her to play the martyr. It also allows her to play with several thousands of pounds a year. Twenty, Regina says. Amanda's the executor of the will. The father knew the youngest — that's Batty — might be put in some sort of institution right after he died. So the bequests, he made were contingent on that." Gillian turned to Jury, her smile sardonic. "I imagine most people could put up with a few pranks for twenty thousand a year, don't you?"

Gillian Kendall did not seem especially cynical. Her face had a wasted look right now, the expression of one who's gone down for the count once too often.

Jury changed the subject. "Who collects the post?"

She looked puzzled. "Well, it depends. I do, Mrs. Lambeth does sometimes; she's our cook. Randolph, who's supposed to be gardener. Carrie Fleet. Whoever happens to be near the post office."

"Did the Baroness Regina ever mention her suspicion that Una Quick was reading people's letters?"

"Oh, yes. I'm quite sure she's right, too. I sent Paul — Dr. Fleming — a note that he was positive had been opened. He laughed about it."

Her face burned. *She* hadn't laughed about it.

Jury asked her point-blank. "What's your relationship with Dr. Fleming, then?"

Another pause. "Nothing." She looked at him squarely. "I'm not sure there ever was."

"That's hard to believe."

She looked away.

"The Baroness says you've been here for about six months. Are you really her secretary or just good company?"

Gillian laughed. "I'm really her secretary. She enjoys having me read her morning post to her. That way, she can hold on to both her cigarette and her coffee, spiked, as you saw, with a tot of gin. As for company, I doubt I'm much company for anyone."

"I'm not having a bad time."

It was the first genuine smile he'd seen from her. "And if you pull that cardigan tighter, I'll be forced to take off my coat and put it around you. Did you see this letter?"

She looked at the one Regina had handed over to him. "*Those* people. Yes, I saw it —" Gillian looked a bit startled. "They can't actually *do* anything about Carrie, can they?"

"No. Extortion isn't held in much esteem by police. Didn't you think it peculiar? Brindle's saying 'the enclosed' ought to be good for another five hundred quid. What was 'enclosed'?"

Gillian frowned. "I don't know. There was nothing." She read the letter through. "I supposed he was talking about the rest of the letter. The trouble and worry — the poor girl'd been attacked, apparently. Doctor's bills —" Gillian shrugged.

"Brindle? From what I can see he's a tuppenny-ha'penny crook. Probably on the dole. Social services would have seen to all that. Well, never mind."

But she looked as if she minded very much, and Jury asked her if she'd heard about Sally MacBride.

With surprising bitterness, she said she hadn't. Jury wondered how many men Mrs. MacBride had got on her list. Fleming, perhaps?

Jury told her, and her look changed quickly.

"*God!* How awful! I didn't know her that well. I've been to the Deer Leap a few times, talked to her a bit, but that's all." She shaded her eyes with her hand, gazed up at the cold blue of the sky. "What's going on in this village?"

"Good question." Jury got up. "I think I'll have a word with Carrie Fleet."

She smiled. "A word is about what you'll get." And she rose from the bench, too.

"You'll lead me out of this maze, I hope."

She looked at him as if she wished she could.

☒

It had once been an arbor, now bricked in, ivy-bound, and moss-encrusted. The stone mason had done rather a sloppy job of it: there were cracks, some of them stuffed with rags against the weather. Though the weather today was fine, a throwback to spring.

The building was long, and at first he saw not her but the wooden crates and metal cages. Some were empty, unused perhaps, or temporarily vacated by their tenants.

Their keeper must certainly have been a virtuoso performer. Cats, dogs, a rooster scratching in the dust, and in the largest compartment — more of a horse box — was a donkey. And on his walk through the grounds he had been startled to see a pony that definitely bore the stamp of the New Forest. It chomped at grass in a patch of woodland behind a statue with a broken arm. It had looked at him for some few moments, apparently used to the occasional two-legged animal, and then returned to its grazing.

Jury's appearance in the doorway caught her by surprise. She had been forklifting hay into the donkey's stall. He tried to remember where he had seen such an expression before; it might have been struck from metal, and that was where he had seen it, on all of the coins bearing the profile of the Queen.

A black and white terrier with a missing leg stayed close to her as she went about her work.

"Now, what's a New Forest pony doing roaming through the woods of 'La Notre'?" Jury smiled.

He was surprised to see her blush before she turned back to the donkey. "It got hit by a car. Tourist, probably," she added without rancor.

"But how did you get it here?"

"Pickup truck."

He leaned against the doorway of the dark hutlike place and simply shook his head. If she shot, no reason to be surprised she drove.

"Doesn't the Forestry Commission take care of them anymore? Those ponies are protected."

"Nothing's protected," she said evenly. She stepped back and surveyed the donkey. "I got him from a tinker. I had to pay him twenty pounds. Him, his caravan, and everything in it wasn't worth that. But I didn't have a gun."

"You usually carry a gun?"

"No. Mostly when I'm in the woods. Poachers, see."

"Most people don't go along with the idea of somebody carrying a shotgun around, you know."

Carrie opened a cage door in which some mourning doves cooed, put in some feed, and turned to look at Jury. "Especially policemen."

"Especially."

There was a long silence. She stood there in her blue dress with a sweater underneath, very straight, like a lightning rod. Jury thought that in that place she was quite firmly grounded. And the longer she looked at him, the deeper the blush. She turned the high color of her face away and took a cat out of its cage. It was a rather ugly black tom with one eye permanently closed.

"Blackstone," she said. Carrie put him down and hunkered down beside him. "Blackstone, come on." There was a combination of command and kindness in her tone. He had heard that quality occasionally in good leaders. The cat didn't move; he seemed afraid to move. She put something a little way away from him. A toy catnip mouse it could have been. It was dusky in the arbor, which had been wired with one bulb. The cat sprang. Carrie smiled.

"I figured he'd have to do something. He was getting pretty bored."

Blackstone flicked the mouse with his paws all round the

dirt floor of the arbor. The terrier watched and then joined in. It was a game.

"Well?" asked Carrie. "I guess you came out here to ask me questions."

"If you don't mind. We could go sit down somewhere."

"I have too much to do to sit." Noisily, she rattled a cage door, trying to open it, disturbing a badger in its rest.

Jury could feel again the turbulence in the air and wondered if it was his proximity that bothered her. He did not think she wanted, as in the case of the tinker, to go for her gun.

"Okay. I don't want to bother you if you're busy. Maybe later."

He turned to go.

"No!" One of the crates toppled and she quickly righted it. The gray fox inside ran round in circles. She smoothed her hands down her dress, brushed her hair over her shoulder, and locked her arms across her breasts. "I mean, go ahead and ask."

Jury smiled. Carrie looked away. "Thank you," he said, with a bit of a try at formality, respecting the distance she put between them. But he was not sure how to go on with her. Not with that look of woe she tried to let pass for either indifference or patience with uncomprehending adults. "First thing, Carrie: you came on the Crowley boys with Miss Praed's cat with a gun in your hands. You don't deny that, do you?"

Carrie hadn't moved her eyes from his, and not a flicker of denial had crossed her face. She was fingering a very small gold chain around her throat.

Jury felt stupid. It was as if he were back in detective training school trying to get a handle on the ways to question witnesses. All he could bring to mind was the stare. Stare the buggers down. They'll come round.

Carrie stared back.

"You shot that gun at them." Jury knew she'd shot it into the dirt. But she didn't bother correcting him.

And still, she'd talked to him about the animals. He'd been stupid, taken the wrong path. "Okay. No one ever poured petrol over me and started lighting matches." Her look shifted like sand. "What'd you have done if they'd gone ahead, Carrie?"

"Shot their kneecaps," she said, reasonably.

"Constable Pasco would have pulled you in pretty quick for that."

"I'm used to him." In an old cage, a finch with a bandaged wing uttered its weak double note. It must have felt there was something worth singing about.

"What's the finch's name?"

"Limerick. Neahle was born there. Before they moved to Belfast." She opened the cage. "You can come out." But the bird still sat, swinging gently on its perch. She closed the cage. "It doesn't like strangers. I guess you're going to do something about the shotgun, aren't you?"

Jury smiled. "I suppose if the Baroness wants a game warden, she has a right to one. It's not up to me anyway, is it?"

To that she simply answered, "I can shoot a gun, too. The Baron liked to hunt and used to do target practice on the grounds. Probably shot off a couple of statues' arms." She put Blackstone back in his cage, along with the mouse.

"Where did *you* learn to shoot?"

"I taught myself. And the Baroness loves to go to Clint Eastwood films. I like the way he holds the gun with both hands." She paused, considering, chewing at the corner of her mouth. "He's handsome, Clint Eastwood." She blushed and shrugged it off. "I mean if you like that type. The Baroness claims the Baron looked like him," she said, hurrying along to cover up her compliment to anyone who might be a policeman. "But I've seen enough pictures of the Baron to know how true *that* is."

"Would you do me a favor and come sit down on that bench?" Jury nodded beyond the opening to the arbor.

"When I'm finished," she said crisply.

Jury smiled inwardly. Might as well try to move a Stonehenge monolith as move her. As she went about her business of feeding her animals, he watched her in the filtered light that cast narrow bands of green across the arbor walls and across her face. Paraphrasing the poem, Jury thought: *A green girl in a green shade*. The poet might have been describing Carrie Fleet, much as she might have hated to be thought a pretty figure in an old romance.

Eighteen

When they were finally seated on the stone bench, with the dog Bingo lying underneath, Jury took out his cigarettes.

"You going to smoke?"

"Do you mind?"

"It's not my lungs."

There was a lengthy silence as Jury smoked and Carrie Fleet meditated. Finally, she said, "For a policeman, you don't talk much."

"For a fifteen-year-old, neither do you."

She shrugged. "Talking's just a nervous habit."

Jury smiled. "Do you mind if I ask you a few questions?"

"No. I'm used to police."

"I understand you've had one or two talks with Constable Pasco."

She bent her head and counted on her fingers. "Eight. Though he makes it out to be more like a hundred and eight."

"That much trouble, is there?"

Now she was gazing at the sky. It was an ice-blue, a frozen-over lake of sky, like her eyes. "Not for me."

"Just for Pasco."

Carrie didn't, apparently, think a response necessary.

"You knew Una Quick and her dog. And seem to know everyone else's dogs and cats. What do you think's been going on?"

"Not accidents."

"Why not?"

She was scuffing the toe of her sneaker in the dirt. "Two dogs and a cat. And two people. That's an awful lot of accidents to happen in a week."

Of course, she would put the cat and dogs before the people. "Have you any ideas?"

"Maybe."

"Mind telling me?"

"Maybe."

Jury looked down at the stub of his cigarette, smiling. "I'd rather question the Queen."

Her blue eyes widened. "Have you, then? What'd she do?"

"Nothing." He laughed.

Interest in Scotland Yard evaporating like the wispy smoke of his cigarette, she sighed and turned away. Jury glanced at her profile — quite perfect, but she didn't know it. The child who'd emerged suddenly was hidden again.

"Given the animals, I guess I imagined you'd have done a lot of thinking about it. Because you'd have cared more."

Still scuffing up dust, she looked away. "Maybe."

This time, the word caught in her throat, one syllable pulling the other along. She turned back. "It's someone in the village."

In the act of grinding out his cigarette, Jury stopped, surprised. "Why do you think so?"

"*Because* —" Her tone was loaded with disgust. "— I don't think somebody would come up from London to poison the Potters' cat or Una Quick's dog. And if I find out who —" The tone was grim.

"I suggest you tell the police."

She just looked at him. Hopeless.

"Have you got a list of suspects, then?"

"Haven't you?"

Jury took out his notebook. "Haven't lived here as long as you. Only got into town yesterday afternoon. Would you mind telling me?"

"Yes, I'd mind." Shading her eyes with her hand, she looked up at the sky. "Probably going to have frost, and I guess that'll please Mr. Grimsdale to death. He can hardly wait to get hounds out. Going to be a meet in a couple of days." She sighed. "It's so much *work*."

"What work?"

Her blue eyes glazed his face. "Unstopping earths."

Jury smiled. "What do you do? Follow the earthstopper when he goes out?"

"Don't have to. I know where they are." She nodded toward the arbor hut and rough-cut wooden sign nailed to it, on which was printed *Sanctuary*. "That's his fox I've got in there. It's a little sick. I'll let it go in a couple of days."

"Good God." Jury laughed. "Can't imagine Grimsdale letting you play nurse."

"I stole it." When Jury opened his mouth, she sighed. "Here it comes. Lecture. It was one of those foxes he bags. If you think it's okay to bag foxes and keep them in a kennel, lecture away."

"No lecture. Does he know?"

"Maybe. But he can't go into my sanctuary. It'd be like trying to drag some thief or someone out of a church."

"If Grimsdale doesn't try, I'd put it down more to fear of broken kneecaps than God."

Her smile was small and faded quickly. He had never seen such a determined chin, such an adamantine gaze. Again, she was fingering the gold chain, its links so tiny they were gossamer. Jury wouldn't have thought Carrie to be much concerned with finery. Part of the necklace was under the jumper, and she drew it out. There was a small ring attached, an amethyst. It was too small to fit her fingers.

"That's very pretty."

She nodded. "I wish *I* had eyes that color."

Jury looked away, smiling. Obviously, she'd seen Polly Praed. "Is it a special ring?"

Carrie held it toward him. "Can you read what's inside? The writing's so small I can hardly make it out. I think my mother gave it to me."

Jury squinted at the initial *C* and the tiny words *from Mother*. He knew she only wanted confirmation, or to share some knowledge that he doubted she herself had. "That's what it says, all right. Do you remember her?"

She shook her head, put the ring back under the jumper. End of subject.

They sat there for a minute, and Jury said, "It would be helpful to know who's going round killing off the animal population."

"And the people," she said calmly. "Una Quick and Mrs. MacBride. I wouldn't be surprised if there's more." Her face turned once again to the sky, as if it were her main concern. "Frost."

Nineteen

*A*manda Crowley was wearing whipcord trousers and a tweed jacket. Jury wondered if she was always scenting, like Sebastian Grimsdale and hounds, for the cold and the frost that foretold the hunt. The Crowley cottage reminded him a little of a rather fancy tack room. It smelled of polish and horses.

It was the first thing she mentioned after the most abrupt of social interchanges. "Hunt starts soon, too bad the boys aren't here." Then she looked about her, as if mildly surprised by their absence.

"Too bad, yes. They've gone back to school, I understand."

"Just two days ago. They'd been on a brief holiday. . . ." Her voice trailed off.

Been sent down, you mean, thought Jury.

"I really haven't much time, Superintendent. I'm expected at Gun Lodge in a few minutes. Can't imagine why you're here, anyway."

Again, he smiled, betraying in Amanda a response she no doubt resented. She fell for it. She pulled down the jumper beneath the jacket and ran her hand, like a comb, over her smoothed-back hair. The body was thin and the hair silvery; still, she would have been attractive except for the creases about the mouth that suggested a crotchety temperament.

"I was wondering how well you knew Sally MacBride." Jury held out his packet of cigarettes.

She took one and rolled it between her fingers for a few seconds, then accepted his match. There was another brief silence. "Scarcely at all. It's a dreadful thing to happen. Poor John."

Amanda crossed her legs. From thigh to ankle, in the tight trousers, it was clear they were well-shaped but taut, like the rest of her. She reminded Jury a little of the riding crop she had absently plucked from the table and was running up and down her leg.

Nicely Freudian, he thought. He wondered how she got on with Grimsdale. "What's 'scarcely at all' mean, Mrs. Crowley? That you spoke to her only to say 'hello,' or 'nice morning'?"

"Well, of *course*, I chatted with her. I often go to the Deer Leap. Don't we all?"

Jury shrugged, rested his chin on his hand, and said, "I don't know, do I?" The tone was mild. No belligerence, except for what she might infer.

"I don't understand all of this. Why are you asking about Sally?"

"What about Una Quick? Now, you *did* know her rather well?"

The little lines around her mouth seemed etched in acid. "*Everyone* knew Una Quick. And I *still* am asking you what's this all about?" She flicked her wrist, looking at the watch with its sensible leather strap, as if she'd give him another one-half minute.

"Gossip," said Jury.

Her eyes narrowed. "I am *not* a gossip, Superintendent. I've better things to do."

"Didn't say you were. But I'd imagine Una Quick was, especially running the post-office stores as she did." Jury looked around the room. Wood-paneled, a couple of saddles — one on a mock-up of a tailor's horse — riding crops, boots, even two brass ones guarding each side of the small fireplace. The glass out of which she'd been drinking was etched with stirrups. "In three days, two accidents. And that's not even mentioning the dogs and the cat. Fatal. Doesn't that make you wonder?"

Her eyes, stone-gray and stone-hard, regarded him. "No, it doesn't. Una had a bad heart; Sally had the misfortune to get trapped in that playhouse." She had the grace to shiver, rubbing her arms up and down. "Probably the wind banged the door shut. Awful to be claustrophobic —"

"You knew she was?"

"*Everyone* knew she was. Was on a train that stalled in the tube and she fainted. Had to sleep with a light on, that sort of thing."

"Don't you think it strange that Mrs. MacBride would be going out to Neahle's playhouse at night?"

Her smile was knowing. "An assignation, perhaps, Superintendent?"

Not much sympathy was being wasted on the dead woman, certainly. "With whom?"

"I can think of one or two. Donaldson, for instance. Only I thought those meetings were generally held at *his* place. And then there's our constable, isn't there? And, perhaps, even Paul Fleming. Too bad for Gillian Kendall."

Jury's jaw tightened. Then he smiled. "Since you're not a gossip, Miss Crowley, perhaps you might know who is."

"Well, I dislike speaking ill of the dead. But certainly Sally MacBride seemed cheek to jowl with Una Quick."

"Ever heard of rumors of Miss Quick's tampering with people's post?"

"Well, Billy and Batty — Bertram — *did* mention —"

She quickly dropped the subject of Billy and Bertram and Jury just as quickly picked it up. "That incident with Miss Praed's cat —"

Her diversion was to say she had no idea who Miss Praed was. "The woman staying at Gun Lodge whose cat was taken from her car —"

Amanda interrupted. "You've been listening to Carrie Fleet, of course. She's hardly to be taken seriously."

"According to her, your nephews were about to burn Miss Praed's cat."

Amanda crushed her cigarette so forcefully it looked like a splayed bullet. "I'm suing that girl for slander."

"You'd have to sue the Baroness. I don't think you'd win. Dr. Fleming saw the cat."

"That *doesn't* prove my boys —"

Jury was losing patience. It was an effort not to show it. "Miss Crowley, I'm not here to press charges about the cat. I'm interested in the deaths of Una Quick and Sally Mac-Bride. And the motive for their murders."

She stared at him through the gloom of the little sitting room. "*Murder?* Their deaths were accidents."

"I doubt that."

"Dr. Farnsworth signed Una's death certificate."

"She was phobic, really."

Amanda shrugged. "I'd hardly call a bad heart that."

"I would. If your behavior was so compulsive you had to call your doctor every Tuesday to report. That's pretty phobic."

Again she shrugged. "I wouldn't know."

Jury got up. "Don't you wonder about your own, Miss Crowley?"

Sharply, she looked up. "My what?"

"Phobia. Cats." Jury smiled and said, "I should be careful, if I were you. Thanks for your time."

She did not bother to rise as he opened the door. Her mouth was still open.

Twenty

The Deer Leap was closed except to guests of the inn and police, though the sanguinity of John MacBride had been replaced, behind the bar, by the sanguinary looks of Maxine Torres.

When Jury asked her for a double whiskey, he almost expected her to say *I don't do windows.* And her sullen though sultry look at Wiggins, who asked for a hot buttered rum, would have been enough to make anyone less determined to stave off a bout of flu forget it.

Maxine was happy to forget it. "Kitchen's closed," she said. "You want beer, gin, whiskey, okay. Sherry, okay. Nothing that means cooking."

"Heating up a bit of water and butter hardly means cooking," said Wiggins.

"Yeah? To me, you have to put it on a stove, it cooks." Even under the heavy lids, the Gypsy eyes stared him down. Then she recited the litany of drinks she would fetch. This time she left out the sherry. She'd have to travel down the bar for that. The optics were directly behind her.

Wiggins gave in. "Brandy."

"Brandy," she repeated, ran a balloon glass under the optic, and plunked it on the bar. All in one motion. Should have been a flamenco dancer, thought Jury.

Wiggins was certain he was coming down with a disease unknown in the annals of medical science. On the way back from Fleming's laboratory, he'd sneezed his head off and asked Jury if there might have been something back there he was allergic to. Only cat or dog dander, Jury assured him, knowing Wiggins could even talk an allergy into something terminal.

He sat beside Jury now, as determined to believe he'd caught something as Maxine Torres was determined not to help him get rid of it. She sat at the other end of the bar, wetting a finger, slowly folding back the pages of a fashion magazine, her interview with Russell apparently not having dented her complacency, and the death of Sally MacBride having turned her attention to a new wardrobe.

The door opened and Polly Praed came in together with a gusting wind that made Wiggins shiver. Maxine looked up, sulking, and informed Polly that the Deer Leap was closed. Respect for the dead. Looking around at the three of them, she made it sound as if only Maxine had any.

"I'm meeting Lord Ardry," said Polly. Jury heard Maxine mumble something, but having taken on the job of temporary publican, she was forced to serve her.

When Polly asked for a sherry, Maxine gave her a look that could stop a tinker's cart, and moved down the bar, Polly calling after her, "Tio Pepe."

"No got," she said, not about to search through the various bottles. She returned with the one nearest to hand, Bristol Milk.

"I don't *like* sweetish sherry."

Maxine shrugged and didn't even look at her. "Don't drink it, then."

"Isn't she a charmer?" said Jury.

Polly braved a look at him in the mirror, adjusting her big glasses. "Oh, hello."

Jury shook his head. "Hello, Polly." He asked Maxine for a pint of best bitter. Fortunately, the beer pull was directly in front of her.

"Hello, Sergeant Wiggins." Her greeting was absolutely sunny. He returned it. "I'm meeting Lord Ardry," she said to the mirror, then let her gaze wander all around the firelit room — at the horse brasses above the bar, at the painting above the fireplace — everywhere but directly at Jury.

"Polly, why don't you stop with that 'Lord Ardry' stuff. You know he dropped the titles." He watched her color and snap open her bag and rummage relentlessly through it, as if looking for proof of Plant's peerage. Looking at his reflection in the mirror, she said, "I can hardly call him Melrose, hardly knowing him as I do. Or don't." She fumbled with her sherry glass.

"Good God. After all the time you spent with him in Littlebourne?"

She was silent.

"You *do* remember your own village, Poll? The murder, the letters —"

"*Poll?* You make me sound like a parrot."

Jury smiled again and shook his head. "You're not nearly so talkative."

It was at this moment that Melrose came down the stairs. He had been looking glum but brightened when he saw Polly.

"Hullo, Polly. Ready for dinner?"

Maxine looked up in alarm.

"Oh, *don't* worry. I wouldn't ask you to boil water."

"I just did," said Wiggins.

ⅺ

"Liberty Hall, back there, isn't it?" Plant was surveying the decor in the recommended restaurant in Selby. The town was charming, the restaurant, or *taverna*, was not — at least in the judgment of Melrose.

"You're always complaining," said Polly equably as she drank her wine.

"I? I beg your pardon. Seldom do I complain. I simply do not care for defrosted *spanakopita*. And this retsina tastes like fish oil" — he made a face as he took another sip — "and I believe all of the waiters and Mama Taverna are really the rest of the Torres family. They're Greek Gypsies." Melrose poked at a stuffed grape leaf. "This reminds me of that horror movie about the body-snatchers —"

"Cut it out," said Jury. "You're putting me right off my meal."

"Sorry. Didn't mean to be rude. I just want to go back to England."

"*I* have to get back to London. Although Racer probably doesn't even know I'm gone yet." He looked at Polly. "I'd pretty much guessed Una Quick wouldn't have made that trek up the hill unless it was damned important —"

Polly looked crestfallen.

"— But the umbrella; that I missed completely."

Polly's violet eyes glimmered. "You can't be expected to notice *everything*, I expect. I write mysteries; I've trained myself to notice things."

"Scotland Yard, of course, hasn't," said Plant, holding up a hand to signal a black-eyed waiter, who was irritated at having his rattling conversation with the other three broken by the customers.

Polly ignored him, chewing a bit of crusty bread. "She'd come out before the storm." Polly frowned.

Jury waited for her to go from A to B. But she only shrugged.

"It wasn't the storm that pulled down the telephone wire," said Plant. "Which means, then, someone tampered with it —"

"*You're* so clever," said Polly, irritably. "That's just what I was going to say."

"Good. Then you would also have deduced that someone knew Una Quick would have to make a telephone call and wanted to force her to walk up that hill."

"That's certainly a chancy way of trying to kill someone," said Polly.

"Like the dog."

"What?" Polly looked suspiciously at the plate of hummus.

"The dog," Plant repeated, asking for the wine list. The retsina had been Polly's idea.

"Don't you agree?" asked Plant, over Polly's head.

"What's this stuff? It looks like something I feed Barney."

"Cats and dogs," said Jury. "The death of that terrier, given the terrible state of Miss Quick's heart, *could* have brought on an attack that would kill her. But it didn't. Next thing, force the old woman right after the poor funeral to huff up the hill to the phone box."

"Still chancy. Polly, will you stop coveting my shish kebab? Eat your catfood."

"Not if there was someone on the other end of the line," said Jury.

Polly reached over quickly and forked a succulent piece of lamb from Melrose's plate, saying, "You mean Una Quick *was* making a call?"

"I'd say she'd been told to call someone at exactly such-and-such time."

"Farnsworth," said Plant. "Everyone in town knew that she called him on Tuesday evenings."

"But that doesn't mean she was calling Farnsworth."

Polly, having helped herself to half of Melrose's plate, stopped chewing and sat back. "What you're saying is that it wasn't a soothing statement about her heart that did it."

Jury nodded. "More likely something quite venomous. Deadly. A threat, perhaps."

" 'I was the one who killed your dog and the same thing is going to happen to you, Una,' " said Plant. "That ought to do it."

"I'd say so. It might have done the job even over her own telephone. But forcing her to physical exertion beforehand would make the result pretty much a dead cert, wouldn't you say?"

Polly, having pretty much polished off Melrose's dinner, was sitting back, wearing her glasses again, staring up at the ceiling. "What an absolutely marvelous way to kill somebody —"

"Really," said Melrose, studying the wine list. "A bottle of blood, Polly, perhaps? Couldn't taste worse than the fish oil."

"No, I mean it —"

"I know you mean it. Here's your moussaka. I'll just have some —"

She slapped his hand away from her plate. Melrose ordered a bottle of Châteauneuf-du-Pape and the waiter, who in truth might have been Maxine's relation, looked at him as if he were crazy. "We got the retsina, house wine, the . . ." He named two or three others.

"Then why is the Châteauneuf-du-Pape on the wine list?"

"Who knows? Have the house wine." He moved off.

Polly continued. "It *is* ingenious. The murderer disguises his or her voice, doesn't get near the victim. So even if it *doesn't* work, the worst that can happen is that Una says she was threatened. And the storm becomes simply a lucky accident for the murderer. Makes it look as if *that's* what knocked out Una's telephone wires, when they'd already been cut."

"Sally MacBride?" asked Polly, well into her moussaka.

"I believe I'll have some shish kebab," said Melrose.

She stared at him. "You just did."

"It would be very much the same thing," said Jury, as

Plant signaled the waiter, disengaging him once more from the interminable conversation going on at the rear of the Taverna. "Probably a number of people knew about that phobia, her fear of the underground, her sleeping with a light on and the door open —"

The waiter had ambled over, yawned, and stared at Plant. "Another shish kebab, if you please."

"You just had some," said the waiter, glaring.

"That's what I told him," said Polly, eyes now on the list of sweets.

"I know I just had some," said Melrose. "Instead of your skewer —" He reached around and picked up his silver-knobbed stick, clicked a button, and the ebony stick disengaged immediately. "Use mine."

The waiter stared at the swordstick and stood back. He gibbered something in Greek and quickly walked away.

"That's illegal," Polly said to Jury.

"Uh-huh. May I go on? A lot of people knew — Sally was a great talker. Gossip would be a better word."

"She was talking about the Underground," said Plant. "'You couldn't get me down there on a bet,' she said. Said the train got stuck once and she nearly fainted. Same thing happened on an elevator."

The shish kebab appeared so suddenly, Jury assumed Plant was right. Everything was pre-prepared. The waiter bore it on a plate, the skewer flaming. He doused the flames, put down the plate, and scuttled off.

"The service has picked up." He speared a cube of lamb and studied it, frowning. "Now, the playhouse. It's very unlikely Sally would have any interest in going there."

"Someone could have persuaded her," said Polly.

"True. Or it could have been done far more easily. Take, just as an example, Grimsdale's kennel master? Or even Pasco? Isn't it more or less general knowledge that Sally MacBride had something going with maybe more than one man in Ashdown? The husband being the last to know. What about a midnight tryst before she leaves?"

"Or," said Jury, "someone sending her a note from one of them. 'Please meet me at the playhouse . . . Vital.' That sort of thing. That little house is accessible to anyone. And screened from the pub. There could be a dozen different ways to get the MacBride woman there."

"But why would she have gone *in* the place? And if she didn't, it wouldn't have looked like an accident."

"If she'd been led to believe the person she was to meet was already there, or would be at an appointed time, she'd have gone in. Too late then."

"You mean the killer is waiting, immediately shuts the door. And leaves."

"Probably. Having knocked off the inside doorknob and taken the bulb from the lamp."

Polly shuddered. "Clever, but God, what a thing to do. Baklava," she added.

"What?"

"My sweet. And coffee." Without a pause, she went on. "The thing is, both of these deaths play on a victim's weakness. Heart. Closed places. The killer doesn't have to *touch* a weapon, so there are literally no traces, except for footprints in the dirt, or something."

"You read too many of your own mysteries. I doubt *this* person would have been so stupid as to leave that sort of trace," said Plant.

Polly glared. "I *never* leave prints in the dirt."

"And what about the other animals — the Potter sisters' cat and the other dog?" asked Plant.

"Red herrings, I'd guess. To call attention away from Una Quick's dog. I wouldn't be surprised if the killer actually thought the death of that terrier would finish her off."

"Funny. If I were going after animals, I'd hit that animal sanctuary of Carrie Fleet's."

Jury smiled. "The *last* place I'd hit would be Carrie Fleet's." He took the letter from Brindle from his pocket. "What do you make of this?"

They both read it. Polly shook her head. "More money?"

Over his gold-rimmed spectacles, Plant said. "What's 'the enclosed' refer to?"

"My question, too."

"Something's been left out," said Plant.

"Taken out, wouldn't you say?" Jury put the letter back in his pocket. "I'm going up to London tomorrow. Take my room at the Lodge, would you?" he asked Melrose.

"Your room? Why?"

"Because I want you to keep an eye on Sebastian Grimsdale, Donaldson, Crowley, the lot. Wiggins is there, but I'd rather have two of you. I mean three of you," he said to Polly's downcast eyes. "Tell Grimsdale about your stag-hunting days."

"*Hunt* a stag. I've never even seen one."

Said Polly, finishing off her baklava. "Just lie. You're good at that."

"Fox-hunting, then. You were up on a horse in Rackmoor. Remember?"

"Very well. Cold toast and gruel is my lot in life."

ж

It was not the maid who opened the door of "La Notre," but Gillian Kendall. "Oh!" She stepped back suddenly.

"I'm sorry. I know it's late."

Gillian smiled. "Not for us. We're more or less night people. But the Baroness is out."

"At this hour? Where's she gone? To the films in Selby?"

Looking rather sheepish and trying not to smile too broadly, Gillian said, "My joke. I meant out like a light. Sorry."

"Why? It was you I came to see, anyway. Lucky for a change."

Somewhat nervously she fingered the row of buttons on the dress she'd been wearing earlier. When she saw Jury watch the fingers, she dropped her hand and blushed.

He laughed. "I haven't come to take you to the nick. You actually look relieved. The guilty flee when no man pursueth. What've you done?"

"Come on in and I'll tell you." She smiled.

Jury stood in the Grecian-English-Italian foyer and said, "I'd rather have a walk. It's a fine evening, and I'm going to London early tomorrow."

"I'd love it. You're not thinking about the crazy maze, are you?"

"Sure." He grinned. "It's probably more interesting at night than by day. I may never make it up to London."

Taking a wool stole from a peg, she said, "I doubt anything could keep you from your job."

The Baron had stationed little lights, hidden really, at different places in his circular maze, and they threw up a dim, unearthly glow on her face whenever she and Jury passed one before winding into darkness again.

"So go on, tell me. Any confession will do."

She tightened the stole about her in the same way she'd tried wrapping the cardigan. He put his arm around her. "Why in hell don't you wear warmer clothes?"

"So people will be tempted to put their arms around me."

"Oh. Fair enough. Let's sit." They'd come to another of the wrought-iron benches. "Go on."

"With what?"

"Paul Fleming. I just wanted to know before I went to London, that's all."

Her head lowered, she plucked the fringe of the stole. "Why? Who's in London?"

In the dark, Jury grinned, thinking of Carole-anne Palutski, trying her best to act the role of pro-tramp. "The most beautiful girl in the world."

It was Gillian's turn to say *Oh*. It was a very sad *Oh*.

His arm around her, he gave her a little shake. "For God's sake, Gillian, you know I'm kidding. There is a beautiful girl. She's nineteen and I'm her father-figure." Jury paused. "More or less."

Laughing and hiding her face in the stole, Gillian said, "Probably more."

"Less. You think I'd take advantage of a nineteen-year-old?"

She looked at him straight. "No. Would you, though, of a thirty-five-year-old?"

They looked at one another for some time, until Jury said, "I think I could give it a go."

The bench was cold and unyielding. Jury wasn't.

When he had carefully looped up each one of the buttons, she said, and he thought it very odd: "It was I, wasn't it, who was supposed to save you from the maze?"

"Like Theseus? The Minotaur hasn't got me. So how do you know you haven't saved me?"

She laughed. It was the first genuine show of joy he'd seen in her. "Oh, it would take a *true* Ariadne for that. Not I."

Jury raised her chin. "Who's the real one, then?"

Gillian thought that over. "Carrie Fleet. She could get you out."

There was for Jury an odd sensation that Carrie Fleet — the way he remembered her standing there in the french door with Gillian at the other one — might be, after all, an Ariadne.

It disturbed him. It disturbed him for no reason he could think of.

But all he said was, "I like older women. Even ones tied in some sort of knot over some other man. I can wait."

He kissed her good-bye.

PART 4

You—too—take Cobweb attitudes

Twenty-one

The Brindles' downtrodden row house on Crutchley Street was not in the moneyed section near the Thames. What prettying up Flossie had attempted had been quickly besmirched by weather, trampling kids, and lack of attendance.

To put Carrie Fleet in this milieu was hard for Jury; it was like a picture with a figure cut out.

Joe Brindle was not at all happy with police on his stoop — to say nothing of New Scotland Yard.

"I won't be long, Mr. Brindle." That was the truth.

Jury wouldn't have sat down even if asked. Though the Brindles were glowering from two tufted lounge chairs, neither of them had suggested he sit. Given an older girl, snoring on the couch-mate of the lounge chairs, there weren't too many choices, anyway. "I just wanted to ask you a few questions about Carrie Fleet. This letter that you wrote to the Baroness —"

With a shaking hand, Brindle put his Bass Ale on the floor and looked at the envelope. "So? We had the care of her all them years, din't we? *We're* the ones found her, wandering round in that woods."

Flossie Brindle wanted her turn. She almost rose from her chair, found it too much effort and went back down again, a diver going for another look at an ocean floor of ale. "A hard case, Carrie was. Never ever said anything; didn't help with the kiddies; only the animals." And as if in a bout of nostalgia — which Jury thought might very well be real — punched her husband's arm and asked, "What *was* that old terrier she fancied so much?" She looked at Jury. "Three legs it had. Can you beat it? Didn't go in much for beauty, did she?" Flossie plumped up her home-permed curls and gave Jury another look at her knees.

Not much for beauty, Jury thought. "The letter, Mr. Brindle?"

Brindle looked at the envelope, shrugged, handed it back. Then he rose from his chair, a little unsteady on his feet, his manner defensive rather than threatening. "Look, that girl was a burden, there's no reason we couldn't ask the old lady for a bit more."

Where Brindle made his mistake was in thinking Jury knew as much as Brindle. "A thousand pounds wasn't enough, Mr. Brindle?"

Joe Brindle's body heaved, the belly protruding even more over the unbelted trousers. *"No!"* He tried to swagger it off. "You come in here, about that little bitch —"

Although Jury's reflexes were usually in control, he knew that if Flossie Brindle hadn't jumped from her chair and thrown the rest of her Bass in her husband's face, Jury would have hit him. *"Fooled around with her, you did. Bloody liar. Thought I didn't know,"* she said to Jury.

Jury supposed he'd known it, but still he felt sick. He waited. Flossie wanted her revenge.

Brindle was wiping the wet from his face, mumbling how he'd never got anywhere. Carrie was too quick for him.

Something to be thankful for, at least. "This letter, Mrs. Brindle —"

Flossie interrupted. "Called herself 'Baroness.' That's a hoot. Manchester or Liverpool's more like it. Well, we neither could believe it. Why would anyone want Carrie Fleet?" She shrugged, lay back again in the dark blue chair, and said, "So Joe, here, he thought why not try for a little more of the ready." She uncapped another bottle.

"Why don't you shut your face, Floss?" His eyes were glazed over; Jury could hardly believe it was from remorse — or any other emotion. He shrugged. "Nothing come of it." And he looked around the room, the pile of dirty clothes a thin cat was making dough on, the snoring girl on the couch, the velvet painting of a deer, as if nothing had come to much.

Flossie, at least, could be counted on for nostalgia, even if it was ale-sodden. She'd taken the letter from its grimy envelope, handwriting like that of a child. "Guess she kept the snap." She took another swig from the bottle.

Jury tensed.

"I'll tell you this," said Joe Brindle. "Flossie here's got a temper, but she ain't no fool." He almost smiled. "Recognized that uniform straightaway, she did." And he gave her a friendly little cuff on the arm.

Jury sat down, smiled, and said, "Do you think I could have one of those, Flossie?" He nodded at the Bass Ale.

There was clearly nothing she'd like better than a chance to serve the superintendent. It allowed her to adjust her legs, the black-patent-leather belting in swells of flesh, and to play Hostess. She even brought him a glass.

"Thanks. I suppose you kept a copy?" Brindle would be smart enough not to send the original off without making one. Or keeping the original and sending a copy. After drinking down half a glass and keeping his smiling eyes on Flossie, he said, "Mind if I have another look?"

"The maid? Yeah, why not." Flossie left and returned with a snapshot. It had curled at the edges, not very clear, apparently taken on a rainy day. There was a young woman, in a dress and cape that might well have been a "uniform," trying to restrain a blur of an Alsatian that seemed much more interested in the nearby gaslight than in her. Her head was back; she was laughing at this trial.

"Amy Lister," said Flossie.

"You knew her?"

Flossie shook her head. "It's on the back."

Jury turned the picture over. The name was printed there. Brindle said it again: "Smart girl, is Flossie."

"Why didn't Carrie take this picture with her?"

Flossie shrugged. "Dunno. Maybe after all these years she forgot it was there. The purse lining was ripped and the snap was in between it and the outside."

She lit a cigarette, tossed the match more or less in the direction of an ashtray, and said through the rising spiral of smoke, "See that lamp? The one the dog's trying to piss on? Well, I knew where that was. It's one of the last gaslights left in England. Off the Embankment it is. And then I got t' thinking." She paused, perhaps to demonstrate that particular power. "See, I used t' work at the Regency Hotel. I waitressed there. That gaslight, it's near the Embankment and right down that narrow street from the Regency." Her eyes grew misty. "The tips you could make. I mean, that Regency! You had to be nearly rich as the Queen —" She pointed her cigarette at the snapshot. "I didn't know her, but that Amy Lister's wearing a maid's uniform from the Regency. You got the money, you could get one of them maids or the porter t' walk your dog. Now, I says t' meself, what's this Carrie Fleet doing with this snap?"

"And you tried to trace Amy Lister?"

Here she gave her husband a smart slap. "Joe here did. Worse luck."

"You went to the Regency?" Jury was looking down at the young laughing woman. A nice person, he thought. Out there on pavements sleek with rain, getting wet herself — well, if Flossie was right, the payment might have been worth it. "Didn't find her?"

For the first time, Joe seemed to come back to the real world. "You don't know sod-all, Super. And you being Scotland Yard." He leaned toward Jury, his ale-laden breath spanning the distance between them. "I took some money, not much — well, we're on the dole, ain't we —"

Jury looked at the video recorder. "I'm sure."

"— and gave twenty quid — *twenty* — to the old coot worked the desk, white gloves and black tie, think the help was all going to a bleedin' ball. Anyway, I paid him to give me the dope on the maid in that picture." Brindle appeared to delight in holding Jury hostage to suspense, for he took the moment to uncap another bottle, light another cigar, blow a smoke-ring.

"Turns out, he couldn't remember her name was Lister, but he did her face. Said far as he knew, she went into service in Chelsea, so I goes *there*. Right proper little bit of sleuthing, 'ey?"

"Depends. What'd you find out?"

Brindle waved the question away with a figure eight of cigar smoke. "Nothing, yet. She'd left, no notice." Furrows of simulated thoughtfulness crossed his brow. "But I ain't stupid. I'll find her."

"That'd be the day." The voice, almost ethereal, as if it inhabited no human form, came from the couch. Jury hadn't noticed the snoring had stopped.

The Brindle daughter had turned. Her eyes looked, through the smoky light, directly into Jury's. "She fed the cat, she did. And she never asked for nothing, and she never tried to put herself in between me and them. Not that there's much between. But Carrie never tried."

The girl — he didn't 'know her name. She was still lying, but leaning on one elbow. A change had come over the room, as if a tomb had opened, the voice of one long dead frightening the living. Directly at Jury she looked, and he saw, to his surprise, she was very pretty. Buried as she had been under coverlets and blankets, he had merely imagined some greasy-haired child, dull and inarticulate.

"I thought about it a long time, that snap," she said, nodding toward it. *"Him,"* — and with a deprecating nod of her head, she motioned toward Joe Brindle — "he never did sort it out. Come back from this Chelsea place, no, couldn't remember no Amy working for them."

Brindle lowered his head.

The look the girl gave Jury was near pleading. "How could they remember? It wasn't the maid. Amy was the dog."

The girl lay back, flung her arm over her eyes, and said nothing more.

Twenty-two

Through the open door of Chief Superintendent Racer's office, Jury could just glimpse the cat Cyril — only his head, since he was sitting in Racer's leather desk chair — carefully washing his paw. The usual mists and drizzle of October had given way to a sunlit afternoon, the light of which beamed through the chief's window and spangled Cyril's coppery fur.

Cyril, unlike his keeper, savior, or whatever one might call Racer's secretary, seemed concerned only that cleanliness, not beauty would get him through those pearly gates. Fiona Clingmore was far more convinced that the art of nail-varnishing was the heavenly priority. More to the nails she was holding up for inspection than to Jury, she said, "He's out."

Jury nodded toward the Racer's door. "Obviously. The Met has been left in better paws than Racer's. When's he coming back?"

That Racer came back at all was a mystery to the Metropolitan Police. At least twice a year there were rumors of the chief's imminent departure, which never materialized. There were even worse rumors that he would be kicked upstairs to an assistant commissionership. Fortunately for the safety of Greater London, the kick never landed.

"He's at his club. Been gone since eleven, so I dunno." Her eyes squinted. She inspected her index finger. A flaw. Carefully, she just touched the tiny brush to the nail. Satisfied, she recapped the bottle and waved her fingers in air to dry them. Now she could concentrate on smiling at Jury.

"You wield a mean brush, Fiona. Matisse wouldn't have stood a chance."

"Had your lunch?" It was a ritual question. Jury always had some excuse. Not that he didn't like Fiona; indeed, she fascinated him in many ways. Right now she rested her elbows on the desk and let the fingers hang down, nails purplish-black like talons. Her lipstick was the same color, which rather washed out her already pale skin. The silvery strands in her blond hair she put down to frosting. Nails dry, she now stood up and took the opportunity to display a laddered stocking, which she turned and presented for Jury's inspection. "And I just bought them." Her half-turned, hand-on-hip position also showed the curve of the hip-hugging black skirt and the beruffled blouse, sheer black like the slightly laddered stocking. Just a tiny one at the ankle that she held up in case his eyes had gone bad in the last three days. Jury loved the way Fiona tried for the demimondaine and only ended up seeming old-fashioned. He could imagine her carefully washing out her undies at night, before rolling up her hair and creaming her face. Suddenly, he felt sad.

He hadn't time for lunch, he told her. She accepted this, as always, with grace.

"He's in a right temper," she said, nodding her blond curls toward Racer's office. "And seeing that cat there won't help it along. *Cyril!*" There would be hell to pay if Racer found Cyril sitting in his own kingly perch. "He says he's going to garrote him."

Cyril paid no attention to commands or to threats on

whichever of his lives he was enjoying. Racer had nearly got him one day with a letter-opener.

"Cyril knows what he's doing. Did the Hampshire police call?"

"Well, they didn't *complain*. I listened on the extension. Of course, he'll say they did." Fiona ran a blank page in her typewriter and called for Cyril again, who just kept washing. She checked her tiny bejeweled watch. "Been down at that club two hours now —"

The subject under discussion just that moment walked in, the tiny red lines on his face rather like the laddered stocking, red turning to blue nearer the nose. Jury guessed about three doubles. And brandy to follow. Savile Row–suited and boutonniered, Racer looked more as if he should have been in a window of Burberry's than in a New Scotland Yard doorway.

"It's Superintendent Jury. Well. I haven't interrupted your little Hampshire holiday, have I?"

Fiona, her face expressionless, was banging her newly painted nails on the typewriter.

"Got those letters done, Miss Clingmore?" he asked smoothly.

"Nearly done," said Fiona, equally smoothly. "Just the finishing touch here and there."

"Well get the here and there into my office quick, girl!" He snapped each syllable out as if he were shooting rubber bands. "Come on, Jury!"

The cat Cyril had slipped like cream from the chair and now lay in wait in the corner under the desk.

As soon as Racer planted his feet there, Cyril slid himself around the knife-pleated trousers, then whipped out and whizzed toward the door Jury had been careful to leave open a few inches.

A few expletives and a paperweight followed Cyril on his way.

"Miss Clingmore! Throw that beast out of the window!"
The Cyril-ritual always ended on this note.

As did the Jury-ritual end on one much the same, except that paperweights and letter-openers were not for him. No fate was mean enough for Jury. Being roasted on a turning spit would probably have been the chief's choice, largely because he thought Jury, rather than Cyril, might be sitting in that leather chair one day.

That Jury would rather sit on a curbstone in a blinding snowstorm did not occur to Racer. Naturally, anyone with Jury's rank *had* to be after the chief's job.

"The Hampshire police are raising holy hell, Jury. Just how did you manage to slip this one over on me?" He did not stay for an answer, but turned on the mental tape that had detailed Jury's egregious errors and derelictions of duty over the years.

"They seem to welcome my presence, actually. Sir."

Racer always noticed the infinitesimal pause and glared at him. "You're larking about in Hampshire investigating a couple of accidental deaths —"

"Maybe."

"Maybe? Even Wiggins can tell the difference between accident and murder. I think."

"I'd like twenty-four hours. That's all. You can surely do without me for twenty-four hours."

That would put him in a bind, thought Jury. Racer had a way of reminding him the Met could do without Jury forever. Into the brief silence where Racer must have battled with this problem, Jury jumped. "I was wondering if you could do me a favor. After all, you have *influence."* The flower girl on the steps of St. Paul's couldn't have plied her wares so well.

"Certainly I do. Would I have got where I am — ?" Then seeing the weevil in the boll of his career, Racer rushed on. "What sort of favor?"

"You lunch at the Regency rather often . . . ?" Rather seldom, Jury knew.

But it worked enough to make the chief superintendent smile his thin-as-a-penny smile. He flicked his lapel, as if a crumb of some privileged repast and all its perks still clung to his garments. "When I've the time. Why?"

"Know anyone named Lister?"

To cover up his obvious lack of knowledge, Racer asked Jury what made him think this Lister would get into the Regency? "You know what sort of place it is. Not just *money* gets you in. Privilege, that's the ticket. And as far as getting information out of the management goes, forget it. Manager'd be on the phone to the A.C. unless ten guests had just been knifed over their Rémy. Or Armagnac."

One thing Racer knew was brandy.

One thing Jury *didn't* know was the name of the manager. Which was what he wanted to know. Jury didn't give sod-all about the manager's calling the assistant commissioner. He just didn't want him or her calling Lister. And given his plan, he certainly hoped it was a man. Too much tradition at the Regency, he was sure, for a woman in that job. "One of the best in London, he is," said Jury, hoping Racer would rise to the bait.

He did. "You mean Dupres?"

"Umm."

"Just how do you know Dupres? Been nosing about?"

No. You just told me. "Heard his name somewhere."

"Georges doesn't deal with People."

Thanks for the first name, thought Jury.

"There's an assistant for that."

"I should imagine. Now, about that twenty-four hours —"

Racer waved his hand. "Hampshire can have you. I've got work to do."

Jury left. As he walked out, the cat Cyril slipped in, gliding noiselessly and almost invisibly across the copper carpet.

×

His first stop was at a costumier's off St. Martin's Lane used by theater people and the rich who wanted to do Marie Antoinettes and harlequins at drunken fancy-dress parties.

" *'Ello*, luv," fluted a voice.

Jury turned to see a youngish woman with fire-brigade curls eyeing him, the eyes outlined in black. She looked as if she was just making up for that party herself. There was a velvet coral band round her neck tricked out with a cameo, and between that and her waist, not much of anything. Slash-and-dash must be the fashion this year, he thought.

"I wanted to hire a costume."

She looked him up and down. "Come to the right place, you did. What sort?"

"Actually, just a few pieces of women's clothing —"

Her smile altered.

"Not that kind, dear. No whips and chains, either."

She giggled. "It'd be hard to believe anyone looks like you —"

Jury broke up that encomium, but still smiled. "I'm stupid when it comes to fashion. Do you have anything that you'd say would look particularly French?"

"Inside or out, ducks?" Her tongue, coral like the band, ran round her lips.

"That's cute. I'm talking about a dress. Dignified but sexy —"

By now she was leaning on the counter, fingers intertwined, chin resting in them. The case housed some spangled masks and Jury wondered if it wasn't rather cold on her breasts, since nothing much supported them except the glass top. She looked at him as if this were absolutely the most fascinating request she'd ever got. "That's a tough one, luv."

He was getting impatient. Running the gamut of female enterprise could be tiring sometimes. But he only smiled more disarmingly. "Not for you, I bet. Say a size —" He gave her the once-over, just to please her. "No, a little bigger."

She leaned farther. "Where?"

"More or less where you're leaning, love."

Again, she giggled. "Ain't you a caution?"

Jury didn't think so and wanted to get on with it. The only problem was the dress and hat. He'd already eyed a short sable cape he wanted. Probably cost him a month's salary to get it for a day.

He followed her through hangered garments and he had to say she knew her business. She judged the size as a ten. "Bust okay?" She held it against her own.

"It certainly is."

Tiny white teeth glimmered at him through coral lips. The dress was a draped crepe de chine, silky green, low-cut waist . . . well, it was hard to find the waist. "Perfect."

He'd decided against a hat; why cover up the hair? "There's a sable cape, short, back there. How much?"

"How long?"

"Half a day, maybe."

She was bagging the dress, wrapped in tissue paper. "We can only rent for a whole day. For you, hundred quid."

"Good lord." He took out his checkbook.

"Oh, you get some of it back. Deposit, see. We wouldn't want just anyone walking off with *that* little number."

He took the parcel and asked her her name.

"Doreen," she said, hopefully.

"You're good at your job, love." Jury took out his warrant card. "So'm I. You don't have to worry about the sable."

She stared. "Crikey!"

Twenty-three

Jury's foot had barely scraped the stone step of the Islington house when the window flew up above him on the second floor, and a bolt was thrown back in the basement flat.

"*Super!*" shouted down Carole-anne Palutski. He looked up.

"*Pssst! Mr. Jury,*" whispered Mrs. Wasserman. He looked down.

Carole-anne was not on the telephone, so he'd called Mrs. Wasserman — for whom the telephone was a lifeline, little as she went out — to make sure Carole-anne was there. Jury had already been ninety-percent sure. Daylight began at noon for Carole-anne.

They both had been eagerly waiting his return. He shouted up to Carole-anne, dressed, or undressed, in her flimsy nightie, to pull herself back in; he'd be up in a minute. Then, carrying his parcel and some flowers, he went down the several steps to Mrs. Wasserman's apartment.

Or fastness, he should say. The bolts thrown, the chain unlatched, all she needed was to lower the drawbridge, metaphorically speaking, to let him in. *To be on the safe side* had little meaning for Mrs. Wasserman, for whom safety was a passing condition, something that quickly faded when she got used to the installation of Jury's last lock or window-guard. Always, she could find another possible means of entrance for the intruder who never came (and, Jury knew, never would). But the Feet followed her, she was sure, when she went out, and had done ever since the Big War.

From her stout, neat frame, today clad in navy blue lawn, came her breathless account of the past few days. Her plump hand pressed to her heaving bosom, she might indeed have been running down long streets, fleeing her shadowy pursuer. Patiently, Jury waited, leaning against the wall, nodding, nodding.

". . . right to keep an eye on *that* one. Such a child she is, innocent, you know what I mean, out at all hours, and, of course, you know I don't go out at night — I apologize, I cannot follow to see she gets into no trouble. . . ."

"I hardly expected you to do that, Mrs. Wasserman," he said to her outspread arms, her look of mournful apology, the failed policewoman who could not keep an eye on her quarry. "I really don't think Carole-anne is getting up to anything."

"Ah!" Mrs. Wasserman closed her eyes in pain. "Would I suggest *that?*"

No, but it wouldn't be a bad idea. He hid a smile.

"And her men-friends — she says they are cousins. But such a large family? Twenty-four she says she is —"

Carole-anne had aged two years in three days. My.

"— but truly she looks only eighteen or nineteen. And her clothes, Mr. Jury." Sadly, Mrs. Wasserman shook her head. "What can you do with one who wears sweaters down to here and *such* tight pants. Like skin, they are."

You can do plenty, thought Jury. "That's why I wanted you to, you know, give her a cuppa, chat her up a bit. . . ." Jury shrugged.

Mrs. Wasserman's small black eyes grew hard. Even her tightly pulled-back hair had a determined look about it, as if she'd nearly pulled it out in thinking about Carole-anne Palutski. "I have had her in for tea or a coffee. And she has kindly returned the favor, though it is difficult for me to walk up three flights. I say nothing against the child; the soul of kindness. Just — what can I say? She says she goes to the films. Every *night*, Mr. Jury? There are not that many films in Islington. You do not think she takes the Underground into the West End . . . ?"

It went on, interrupted only by Jury's handing her the bunch of roses he had picked up outside the Angel tube station. "You're doing a good job, Mrs. Wasserman."

She was overwhelmed. "For *me*? Roses." She might never have seen one in her life. And she was spieling off her thanks in Czech or Lithuanian — Jury remembered she spoke four or five languages.

French. Jury smiled. "Would you do me another favor?"

"*You* ask *me*? After all that you have done for me. Name it," she added, with a sort of special-agent crispness.

"You speak French."

Her eyebrows slanted upward. Didn't everybody?

"Mine's very rusty, what I ever knew." He had his hand on the door. "Would you mind staying in for a half-hour, an hour? I'm bringing Carole-anne down."

He had asked her if she'd "mind" only to give her whatever spurious support there was in his thinking she was free as a bird, one who flew at will all over Islington, London, wherever.

"Indeed I wouldn't, Mr. Jury. But why this French?"

"You'll see." He smiled. "Bet you don't recognize her."

x

Jury certainly did. It was mostly naked skin that had hung over the windowsill, and although it was now covered, it made no difference. The body would turn a suit of armor to a pane of glass. There was just no way of hiding Carole-anne.

She threw herself at him as if he might be one of the many long-lost fathers, brothers, cousins that had accumulated on the stairway over the past weeks. "Super! How's about a kiss, then?"

"Sure," said Jury, giving her one right on her soft lips. "Oh, cut it out, Carole-anne," he said, dragging her up from the floor and out of a pretended swoon.

"Nearly fainted at that one. Let's have another go." Before he could stop her, the arms were like steel bands around his neck, and she seemed to have maneuvered parts of herself into every crevice of his body.

He pulled her arms away. "You kiss your dad like that?"

Meltingly, she looked up at him. "Ain't got one. Just you. Dad." And she tried it again.

He shoved her back. "Who're all these men been trailing up and down the stairs like a school of sharks?"

Carole-anne's already pink cheeks turned crimson, as if she'd just dabbed on rouge. "You mean *she* told you?" She pointed toward the floor. "Well, bloody damn. I never —"

"Mrs. Wasserman only told me you had a brother and a father. She thought that was very nice. Thought you were being taken care of."

The fire that flared, died. "Oh. Well, had to tell her *something*, didn't I? So bleedin' innocent she is. Nice old bag o' bones, but she sticks to that flat like glue. I did what you said and got her up here for tea and biscuits." Carole-anne's mouth puckered. Tea was not her drink. "So she couldn't come up here, so I go to her place. Tried to get her to come down the Angel pub with me, but you might as well try to get the street lamps to walk —"

Jury burst out laughing. Mrs. Wasserman going down the pub.

Carole-anne was miffed. All her good work should have rated more than a laugh. "You did a great job, love. She likes having you round. Puts some life into this old pile of bricks, she said."

"Oh. Well." Carole-anne sat down beside him. "Lay on a cig, Super, okay? I'm out."

No matter what she said, it sounded like sex. He got out his pack of John Players, lit one for both of them, and said, "I've got a job for you, Carole-anne."

"How much do I have to take off? I stop at —"

"I don't want to know what you stop at. Actually, this involves putting *on* clothes." He'd been unwrapping the parcels, and when she saw the sable she shot up from the sofa. "And there's some money in it for you, Carole-anne."

With her eyes glued on that sable, she said, "There's some positions I don't do, and no ropes and tie-ups —"

"Shut up!" He knew she talked like that just to get a reaction. Carole-anne Palutski probably hadn't gotten many reactions that didn't have a tab on them. It came to him with a small shock, that thought. For a brief moment, his command had penetrated the Glo Dee Vine mask, and he saw what Mrs. Wasserman saw, however misled her vision of it. Carole-anne looked innocent.

He thought of Carrie Fleet and his blood ran cold.

"Work, love."

A half-hour later he was tapping his coded knock on Mrs. Wasserman's door, and he had to admit, he didn't think he'd have recognized Carole-anne Palutski himself.

Of course, she looked gorgeous, as he'd known she would. Though the dress was draped, there was still that tiny strain across the bust, but the rest of it hung in such gentle undulations that the body underneath was plainly not advertising.

Jury thought of Gillian Kendall and tried to brush that thought away. But it was the paint job that was a marvel. Nothing flamboyant, she had gone at that makeup case with the eye of a surgeon. Outliner like a scalpel, lip-liner incised. Blusher like the real thing. Absolutely perfect. To top it, she looked ten years older than the ages she'd been doling out.

"French?" she squealed, on their way downstairs. "You crazy?" But her eyes and hands were all for that sable cape.

"Mr. Jury! What a surprise!"

It was. Mrs. Wasserman stared at Carole-anne with squinty eyes, eyes trying to adjust themselves to a totally different light. "How do you —?"

"Hey, babe," said Carole-anne, chewing inexorably away at the gum Jury told her she'd have to park beneath a bench or behind her ear.

"Carole-*anne?*"

Carole-anne was pleased at the shock of recognition. "One and," she said. "Come for the lesson. Only French I know is *bonjour.*"

Mrs. Wasserman smiled. "You pronounce it that way, dear, they will think you are Japanese."

Carole-anne giggled. "You're a right caution sometimes." Then, from her queenly height (fortunately, she'd had the right shoes) she deigned to look at Jury. "*He* thinks I can learn to talk like a frog in ten minutes."

"Right now you talk like a frog, dear. But French, you do not sound."

Carole-anne giggled again. They must have been getting on like a house on fire.

Mrs. Wasserman fluted, "*Bonjour, monsieur. Il y a a long-temps, Georges.*" Arms folded, she looked hard at Carole-anne. "Repeat, please."

Carole-anne had parked the gum. She repeated.

"Again."

Again.

" 'Il faut que je m'en aille.' Repeat."

Carole-anne did so.

"Again. Three times."

Three times.

After a few more phrases and few more repeats, the lesson was over.

"Thanks, Mrs. W.," called Carole-anne, as the bolt shot home behind them in the basement flat.

Jury had reckoned on an hour. A phrase here and there. It had taken only fifteen minutes.

No wonder Carole-anne wanted to be an actress.

Twenty-four

ury had parked the police car illegally near the Charing Cross Station, and Carole-anne reminded him he'd get a ticket. He handed her a card.

"A bloody baroness. Wherever did you get this? Is this me, then?"

"For the next hour. Then the coach turns back to a pumpkin."

"You call this a coach, Super?"

He helped her out of her side of the Ford and watched, as they walked the two blocks down the narrow street, the looks of the men. And of the women, too. But the men tended to stop dead. Some of them were wearing bowlers.

Carole-anne could have stopped a beer lorry in the middle of the M1. She didn't even seem to notice the effect she was having. Then Jury noticed her lips were moving. Probably in the silent gutturals of the *r*'s that Mrs. Wasserman had so easily rolled from her throat.

In the marble foyer of the Regency, which was an unpretentious-looking, narrow building with only a brass plaque to bear witness to its name, a name that could be singled out by the select — which certainly didn't include C.S. Racer, but miracles would happen. On its opposite wall outside was one of those little blue plaques which announced that a famous writer had written his classic novel on these premises. (A page of it, perhaps, thought Jury.)

There was, in the foyer, one of those old-fashioned sedan chairs in which now dozed the doorman. But he came to right swiftly when the door whished shut behind them.

Carole-anne whispered, "Bleedin' morgue, it reminds me of."

"Quiet," said Jury, wondering if this could possibly work.

He felt almost remorseful for underestimating Carole-anne's powers of persuasion. He certainly hadn't underestimated the effect she had on the young man in white gloves behind the rosewood desk. At her *Bonjour, monsieur,* and its accompanying smile, the pen with which he'd been filling in something in a daybook stopped in midair.

"Ah, my'ah Anglais, ees not, you know, *perfect.*" Here came a tiny, deprecating shrug, as she handed him her card.

The bow dipped his head nearly to the counter. "Madame." Meltingly he looked into her sapphire eyes. "If I could be of service." Jury might as well have taken his place among the palm fronds and the marble statuary. If any question arose, he was to be her uncle.

"*Mon ami,* I weesh to speak with my old, ah, friend, Georges Dupres. He ees, how you say, manager?"

The young man — at least young, Jury thought, for the high-powered job of assistant manager at the Regency — seemed at a loss. "Madame! Please forgive me, but . . ." And then he flew off into a torrent of French as Carole-anne arranged her décolletage more winningly over the counter and looked sad.

What in the hell the fellow was saying, Jury didn't know, and was afraid this would dish it right here —

No. Carole-anne put her hand, in what might have been a forgiving gesture, on his arm. Jury was sure her eyes were silvered over with tears, given the way the assistant manager looked at her. She shook her head, she sighed, she said, turning to Jury, *"Mon oncle."*

And then she went to sit on a damask dais, removing from her small bag a lacy handkerchief.

Mon oncle went over to her, smiling sweetly, patting her on the shoulder, and saying, "What the hell are you doing?" It was out of earshot — though lord knew the way he stared at the new Baroness Regina de la Notre, the assistant manager might have had far-reaching antennae.

Through her brimming eyes, Carole-anne smiled soulfully up at Jury and said, "Why bother with George-bloody-Dupres? Not with this other one locked up."

She rose, she turned, she waved a sad farewell and, to Jury's amazement, started toward the door.

The assistant manager might have been wearing electric shoes, the way he sprang from behind the desk and grabbed her arm. Then let his hand fall, aware that he might have contaminated a guest of the Regency. "If there is some way *I* can be of assistance, madame?" Oh, the look of hope.

"How kind of you," said the baroness, throatily. And then mumbling, ". . . *il fait un temps* . . ." Carole-anne shook her head, probably wondering how to use up her short supply of French phrases.

"Anything, madame."

As if it were but a sudden inspiration, she snapped her leather-gloved fingers, and drew from her purse the picture of the servant and the dog. Jury didn't think there was much chance of the *assistant's* going back eight years but what the hell?

The man could barely take his eyes from Carole-anne long enough to glance at the picture. He shook his head and said he was sorry, but . . .

"Ah, ees the, how you say, livery of the Regency. Uniform. She was maid? Waitress? *Non?*" Carole-anne flipped the snapshot over. *Amy Lister.*

To Jury's surprise, the penny dropped. It was gratitude more than surprise that registered in the assistant manager's face. He remembered. He even allowed himself a chuckle. "Of course. The Listers." Then he looked like a chicken with its head in the wringer. He'd got the Listers straight, but . . . "It wasn't the maid you were wanting? You're right, that is our livery, but I've never seen the maid. Only the dog, the Alsatian. It was always with the Listers. That's what I remember."

Carole-anne gave him such a lovely look as she shook her glowing, chignoned head, that he started rattling on about the Listers. He stopped rattling when he saw her drop her head in her hand —

For Christ's sake, Jury wanted to shout. He's telling me what I want to know. What are you on about —?

Again, Carole-anne put her smooth little hand on his arm. "Ah, *mon ami* . . ."

She was going to do that stupid phrase to death. He felt like trampling on her tongue. He stood there, instead, her smiling *oncle*.

". . . eet ees the Baron Lister I look for —"

Oh, bloody hell! The silly little twit was so much into her role she didn't even know why she was there anymore.

The manager looked confused, sad, displeased with himself for not being able to produce the Baron Lister. "I'm most dreadfully sorry. Far as I know, there was never a *Baron* Lister. Would Lord Lister do?"

Lord Lister. Address, Carole-anne.

Her smile was small, sad. She raised her gorgeous face to the heavens and said, *"Si."*

Si? Oh, wonderful.

Blushingly, she changed it. *"Oui.* Myself, *mon ami,* I travel so much, I sometimes forget which country I am in." A batting of thick eyelashes went with this.

Jury envisioned the coast of Spain. Ocean. Shoving the Baroness Carole-anne right into it. Inwardly, he laughed at himself. What he really wanted was to see Carole-anne in a bikini. What the hell was she doing now?

She had handed the assistant manager a tiny address book. He was writing in it, sending up furtive looks to those jewel-like eyes. He nearly clicked his heels as he handed it back. "Ma'am!"

Jury felt if he didn't sit down he'd fall down at this breathless leavetaking. How'd she got his name?

"Henri. *Mon ami* . . ."

I'd rather talk to Racer.

". . . *Vous serez toujours dans mon souvenir.*"

Henry swayed and as she called over, flutingly again, to *Oncle Ricardo*, Jury again imagined the Costa del Sol. But Uncle Ricardo, having done nothing at all, merely smiled, and said, together with the baroness, *"Bonjour, mon ami."*

It was all of that thinking of Sunny Spain that had left him sun-mad, he knew. She sat there, gibbering away in the car and jouncing her gorgeously stockinged leg, and poking him in the ribs.

"So how'd I do, then, Super? We got the goods, right?"

"We did, *mon amie.*"

Mrs. Wasserman was peeking through her heavy curtains. Jury wouldn't have been surprised if she'd been watching out ever since they'd left.

Carole-anne scooted from the car and down the stairs to the basement flat, Jury following.

"Bonjour, madame," said Carole-anne, unwinding her sable cape with a bullfighter's expertise and dropping it on a

convenient chair. " 'Ello, Mrs. W. Lemme get these bleedin' heels off. I could drop where I stand."

Mrs. Wasserman clasped her hands together, looking at her star pupil. "You did well, Carole-anne?"

"Perfectemente. Right, Super?"

"Perfectemente."

Carole-anne, shoes off — and apparently dress coming off, before Jury stopped her — said innocently, "But I thought you had to get this stuff back to the false-face store." She stopped in the middle of unzipping.

"Later, Carole-anne. Right now I have to get *myself* into Lord Lister's good graces and back to Hampshire."

"You was to take me to din-dins, Super," she said, pouting.

Mrs. Wasserman gave him a look that might have been scathing, but she snatched it away.

"I'll take you to din-dins when I get back. Keep the gear"— Jury was writing on the back of one of his cards — "and tomorrow, love, go to this chap. *Adios, señora, señorita.*"

He could hear the gaggle of voices as he ran up the steps. ". . . a bloody the-*at*-rical person. 'Ere now, Mrs. W. Is he pulling my leg?"

"Never would Mr. Jury do that . . . but he might like to . . . ."

Their mixed laughter could be heard even as Jury got into his car, smiling. It was the first time he'd heard Mrs. Wasserman return to her girlish, giggling youth. *Bless your heart, mon amie*, thought Jury, pulling away from the curb.

✕

Before he went to Woburn Place he called New Scotland Yard and got a run-down on Lord Lister: Aubrey Lister, granted a life peerage in 1970, chairman of the board of one of London's most powerful dailies until he retired ten years ago.

⊠

And Jury sat at a red light, engine idling, thinking his brain was too as he looked up the road marker on the side of a building.

Fleet Street.

Some part of Carrie's mind had unearthed, like a fox's covert, that scrap of memory. Though she must have no idea why she'd chosen a name that everyone in London connected with the world of newspapers.

Jury put his head on his overlapped hands on the steering wheel while the Mercedes behind him got very impatient.

Twenty-five

The house in Woburn Place looked as if it had remained unchanged through decades of Listers, kept to its original brass fittings, its stained-glass fanlight, newel post, rosewood table in the entrance-room sitting on a Belgian carpet so silky it reflected the dim light. The room's only concession to the present was converted gaslight, frosted tulip lampshades, the fixtures within now electrified.

The maid who admitted Jury was dressed in starched pearl-gray and a lace cap. It was to her he had shown his warrant card — just routine, of course, he'd said. He'd like a word with Lord Lister. The maid had been well trained to register no surprise. Vagrant, Minister, Scotland Yard — whoever appeared on the stoop at Woburn Place would be dealt with calmly. Still, looking up at Jury she had to adjust both her expression and her Victorian cap. "Have you a personal card, sir?" She smiled.

"Sorry. Of course." Jury dropped one of his cards on the salver on the marble table. She nodded. "Shan't be a moment, sir."

Whatever the maid's origins — the fens, the North, Manchester, Brighton — traces of that accent had been overridden by the West End. She had gone into a double-doored room on his left, carefully pulling them shut behind her.

In a moment she reappeared. It was almost a smile of relief she gave him, while telling him that Lord Lister would see him now.

If it was merely a conferred, a life peerage, one would never have known it from the demeanor and bearing of Lord Lister. No matter he was a smallish man, thin and drawn and in his seventies, his confidence spread, like the fan of sunlight coming through the high windows behind him. And he was, as all powerful men would have you think, a simple man.

"How interesting, Superintendent. Haven't a dog's notion why you're here, but it makes a change. Tea?"

He did not wait upon Jury's acquiescence. Lord Lister pressed a button on one side of the marble mantelpiece.

"Thank you. I could use it." He doubted Aubrey Lister was a man who wasted his time over small talk. "It's about this snapshot, sir." Jury took the snap, creased by now, from his pocket and handed it over. "Nothing that's a police matter, maybe. Only, I'm interested."

Lord Lister, who had reseated himself on a sofa covered in watered silk, took out a spectacle case and said, "Not a police matter." He smiled over his spectacles. "Yet here you are, Superintendent."

Jury smiled. "We lead other lives, Lord Lister."

Jury had caught the old man before he'd barely glanced at the picture. His tone was kind, but he said, "Then we should not lead them on police time, should we?" The corners of his mouth twitched.

Jury was glad he was enjoying himself. He did not want to upset this man, living here alone as he did — if one discounted a plethora of servants belowstairs. But he especially did not want to upset him on the errand on which he had come.

"I'm sorry. I do not recognize this picture. Should I?"

"Not necessarily. I was hoping you would." Jury immediately put out his hand for the snap, pretty sure the snapshot would be withdrawn. And that his lordship would look at it more keenly.

"Turn it over," said Jury.

Lord Lister adjusted his spectacles as if that might clear the cobwebs from his mind. " 'Amy Lister.' " He looked up, his glance around the room leaving out Jury, falling on the mantelpiece and a small collection of gold-framed pictures. Then at Jury. "You've found *Carolyn?*"

"Sir?" All Jury could do now was play the innocent.

"My granddaughter, Carolyn. Amy was Carolyn's dog. This is Carolyn's Alsatian. And the woman —" He shrugged. "A servant of some kind. What do you know about Carolyn?"

"I'm not sure I know anything."

Lord Lister tapped the snapshot. "Then how'd you come by this?"

The tea was delivered by the amiable, if starched, maid. The maid poured, asking Jury how much sugar he desired.

"A couple named Brindle found a little girl years ago in a wooded area on Hampstead Heath, dazed. They'd gone there for a picnic. She didn't seem to know how she'd got there, who she was. All she had was a small purse containing a few pence and this picture. And a very bad head wound."

Lord Lister was clearly shocked. "We supposed she'd been abducted. You're suggesting someone tried to kill her?"

"I don't know."

Lister looked again at the snapshot. "I wonder why the person responsible didn't take the picture?"

"It had got between the lining and the purse itself. The Brindles only found it recently." Jury put down his cup. "When was the last time you saw Carolyn?"

His chin rested on the hands overlapped on his ivory-knobbed cane. "When her nursemaid had taken her to the zoo. In Regent's Park." His sharp eyes looked across his cane at Jury. "The nursemaid returned empty-handed."

A rather sardonic attitude to take toward the disappearance of a child.

"You didn't report it to Scotland Yard, and you kept it out of the papers. How —?" At Lord Lister's tight smile, Jury remembered. The "how" would have been quite easy for the old man. He was chairman of the board of one newspaper and influential with others.

"Penny dropped, Superintendent? How do you think I got my peerage? Apparently, the Queen thought I had done the country some service by keeping a series of especially grisly crimes, the plans of certain drug dealers, and so on, out of the newspapers. I have a certain — influence." His smile was thin. "My son, Aubrey junior, was miffed that the title would last only for *my* lifetime. I told him if he wanted a title, he could damned well go out and get his own."

"You thought that spreading Carolyn's disappearance across the paper would work against her being found — so no reward was offered."

Had there been, Flossie and Joe would certainly have turned up with Carrie in tow.

"Of course, that's what I thought. And I did not want to contact police for the same reason. Kidnappers are rather . . . touchy on that point. That was quite clear when the ransom note appeared two days later. The kidnappers weren't especially greedy. They only asked for twenty-five thousand. Which I delivered personally to the Left Luggage place in Waterloo Station tucked into a suitcase full of clothing. And the stub I left in a paperback mystery in a W. H. Smith's. At the end of the stack. I assumed I was being watched all the time."

"But Carolyn wasn't returned."

"No." He pinched the bridge of his nose and shook his head. "Nor was the money ever collected. I immediately hired two very good private detectives. They turned up nothing. Apparently, the kidnappers did not want to take the chance of showing up. Perhaps Carolyn was already dead. Perhaps —" Lord Lister shrugged. "— anything."

"And the maid, or nurse? What was her story?"

"She'd gone to get them both a cold drink. It had taken only a few minutes, but when she returned, Carolyn wasn't there. She grew more and more afraid as she searched. Carolyn never wandered off, and the servant felt sure she'd been abducted. Straightaway, she came back to the house."

Jury had taken out his notebook, and Lord Lister said, "Oh, don't bother. The nurse is dead. She can't help. She was fired on the spot, of course."

"Did Carolyn's parents go along with your plans?"

"Parent. Carolyn was illegitimate. The father is dead. My daughter Ada is dead, too. Died when Carolyn was three or four. I thought she should have a name."

"It does help one's sense of identity."

Lister looked at Jury sharply. He had not touched his tea. Still with his hands on the cane, he turned his eyes toward the high window, and spoke like a man from whom most emotion had been wrung. "They're all gone, the children. Didn't find the house too — salubrious. Ruth and Aubrey. My sister Miriam finally left, too."

"Gone where, Lord Lister?"

"They do not keep in touch. The last I heard from Ruth, she was —" His glance traveled around the room, came to rest on the pattern in the Oriental carpet. "India, I think. Miriam. I should like to see Miriam again." He looked up, thoughtfully. "We were close, though she was some fifteen years younger."

"Have you pictures of them?" Jury nodded toward the mantelpiece.

He shrugged. "Help yourself. Those are very old."

Old and faded and rather fuzzy. There was one who certainly looked like Carrie. "Her mother?"

"Ada. Yes." Lord Lister seemed disinclined to deal in the past. He looked at Jury. "You think I was a tyrant, that I drove them away?" He sighed. "My dear Mr. Jury, they are merely waiting for me to die." The thin lips pursed. "Money, Superintendent, money."

"People like that usually keep very much in touch. So you'll know where to send it."

Lord Lister actually laughed. "Oh, I like that. No. They know they're going to get it. What's eating at them is that Carolyn is getting the lion's share."

That surprised Jury. "You were fond of her."

The statement seemed to have to pass, like a memo to the board, and come back with stamps of approval. Lord Lister took a long time considering. "Yes. I was fond of her. You see, I felt a bit like Lear. Not that I would hold a mirror to her lips to see if she lived still." His eyes, when they looked at Jury, were like polished silver. They were glazed with tears. "But Carolyn, unlike the others, never *wanted* anything from me. Aubrey and Ruth are selfish and shallow and opportunistic. Actually, Carolyn took after me. And Miriam, perhaps. Resolute. Undemonstrative. Stoic, really. Her mother was like that." He leaned toward Jury, as if he felt it were important the superintendent understand: *"That* is simply something I was never used to. Greed was the major component in the makeup of the other children."

"May I ask how much money is involved?"

"You may. For Carolyn, a million."

Jury stared.

"For the others, a hundred thousand apiece. If Carolyn *is* dead . . ." He looked away. "Then her part of the inheritance would go to them. Evenly divided. But there must be proof of actual death. If she is declared simply legally dead, her inheritance will go to several charities."

So the others would be waiting not only for the death of the old man, but the death of Carolyn Lister. "I don't imagine that made Carolyn overly popular with your son and daughter. And your sister."

A glimmer of a smile. "Not precisely."

"But Carolyn disappeared over seven years ago. Wouldn't that suggest she's dead?"

"Yes. Except that now you've turned up with that picture, haven't you? The young girl who had it *could* be Carolyn. The tale you relate of this family finding her would fit the facts."

"You have other pictures — of the family?"

Lord Lister shook his head. "Of my wife, quite a few. And the children when they were very young." He looked toward the ceiling. "An album, perhaps, somewhere in the attic. I do not go into attics, Superintendent. Like the mind, they tend to be dark and filled with cobwebs. I am not a sentimental man." He paused. "Is the girl you refer to happy?"

Jury thought for a moment. "It's hard to say. But I doubt one could be very happy who has no memory of her childhood."

"Ah. Is she well provided for?"

"Yes."

"Good." He shrugged. "Unfortunately, there is no proof. . . ." He looked at Jury, then around at the luxury of velvet draperies, Georgian furniture, less resplendent now in sunlight grown sluggish. He smiled that thin smile — not so much insincere as one learned from years of dealing in confrontation. "That's up to you, Superintendent."

"She wears a ring, a small amethyst. That mean anything to you?"

Lord Lister leaned his chin on his hands and thought. "Amethyst. I am not positive, but I believe her mother might have given Carolyn one. A birthstone. Yes, that would serve as proof, I'd say."

Proof? "That she's alive?"

"Or dead."

Jury felt a sudden chill. "And if this girl is Carolyn. And if, by some chance, something should happen to her —"

Lord Lister raised his eyebrows. "Unlikely. She'd be quite young now."

"She was quite young when she was left for dead on the Heath," said Jury bitterly.

The old man said nothing.

Jury went on. "Why wouldn't part of that fortune go to the person who's been taking care of her — not the Brindles. I mean the one she now lives with?"

"I suppose it could." Lord Lister seemed puzzled.

Jury waited for the questions. *Who is taking care of her? Where?* . . . But there were no questions. Jury put away his notebook and thanked Lord Lister for his time.

With the help of his cane, the old man rose. "Of time, I have aplenty, Mr. Jury.

Jury smiled. "Then if she were to come here, perhaps your memory would bestir itself. Perhaps hers would. I imagine, living alone as you do, you'd be happy to have her back."

"You don't understand, Superintendent. I do not like attics. I do not want the past back. I do not want Carolyn."

After the pleasant maid saw him out, Jury stood for a few seconds on the stone step. All for nothing. He had done nothing to help Carrie Fleet, who, in a sense, had no past. Million quid or no, she had been truly swindled. He himself could have gone to the attic, taken whatever mementoes he could find, perhaps helped her piece it all together.

But how do you do that when the end of it is that no one wants you back?

He went down the steps and saw, as he turned, a velvet drape drop back in place.

Shutting it all out.

PART 5

Now it is Night—
in Nest and Kennel—

Twenty-six

Melrose — now "on" as Earl of Caverness — stared up at the picture of Grimsdale, in the forefront with a few of the favored staghounds. In the background was a stag at bay about to be taken. And beneath this, and above the mantelpiece, was a hunting horn.

Melrose had a great deal of difficulty in looking at it, much less with admiration. But a job, he supposed, was a job.

"Absolutely nothing like it," said Sebastian Grimsdale, standing beside Melrose Plant in the Lodge's trophy room. Grimsdale sighed with pleasure. "Prince of Wales killed a stag by sweeping the knife upward. Instead of merely slitting the throat."

"That is certainly a lesson in the art of venery, Mr. Grimsdale. It must have been a wonderful sight."

Grimsdale started, slapped his hand on his thigh, and laughed. "Well, I'm not quite *that* old, sir." He grew more serious, as if almost reluctant to say, "Even if I'd been there, I wouldn't have got near the stag. Too dangerous, you see."

"Oh. Sounds a bit like a bullfight to me."

"Good God, Lord Ardry. That's not *sport.*"

Melrose lit a cigar, offered one to Grimsdale, who was so lost in the picture that he merely shook his head absently. "Never done any stag-hunting, then?" Melrose shook his head. "Nothing like it," he said again. "I remember one sprang up from the heather under the very nose of my horse. Ah, well . . ."

There was a pause for nostalgic reflection. "Season's over in Exmoor now for stag-hunting. But if you're here again in the spring —"

"I rather doubt it," said Melrose, trying on a smile. Looking at the stag at bay, the smile didn't quite fit.

Grimsdale noticed the weak reflection of a smile. "Oh, oh. You've been taken in by all that old Landseerian rubbish, *Monarch of the Glen* — sentimental nonsense. They're a nasty sort of beast, the stag. Do you know, one would push another out to take his place, if he was being hunted down."

"Really."

"Absolutely." Grimsdale seemed determined to convince him that the stag was not a family man. "Push out another and lie right down in its place in the heather. Or mingle with hinds. No scruples."

"None."

"None," repeated Grimsdale in a satisfied way. "Too bad you've not hunted stag. Hills, huge distances, awful streams, bad weather —"

"Sounds inviting."

"Well! If the Devon-Somerset pack's out, at least you can hunt with the Buckland. New Forest. Fallow deer, there. Nothing to compare with the red." Grimsdale checked his watch as if the hunt might begin at any time. "Nearly ten. Donaldson will be doing his rounds. Trying to start my own pack of staghounds. Those two staghounds you saw, handsome brutes, drafted those from one of the best foxhound kennels —"

"You've got your own pack of foxhounds. I should think that would keep you busy enough, Mr. Grimsdale."

Whatever hint of disapproval there was in Melrose's tone was lost on Sebastian Grimsdale, who simply said there could never be enough hunting.

Melrose could see that. He was surrounded by the efforts of more than one taxidermist — he doubted *one* taxidermist would have had the time, even if he'd had the interest in working in so many different media: gray fox, pheasant, woodcock, badger — a few of the smaller displays. All under glass. While Grimsdale was lost in wonder at the larger of the mounted heads of stag and buck, Melrose picked up one of the glass cases, looked at the blue-tipped wings. Beautiful bird.

Grimsdale turned. "Ah, I see you like birds, Lord Ardry." The tone suggested that Lord Ardry *must* have a passion for some sort of gunplay.

Alive, yes.

"Shoveler drake, that is. Hardly ever see one in these parts. It's when the weather gets so bad up country they want a warmer climate." Grimsdale gazed at the drake with satisfaction, rubbing his pipestem against his cheek.

"This one found it, I guess."

The sarcasm fell wide. Grimsdale picked another bird, mounted on a a limb, from the mantelpiece. "Teal. Dozen of them took off from the pond —"

"Pond? I didn't see one."

"Round back." Grimsdale laughed. "Not supposed to see it, Lord Ardry. Just luck it was there, surrounded by trees, bracken, rushes. Absolutely perfect. I keep the mallard there. That draws the others."

Melrose was eyeing the shoveler drake, sorry for it, but feeling he'd warmed up Grimsdale enough, both with brandy and talk, to get round to the real subject.

"Hunting and shooting's not my line —"

"Worse luck for you, sir." Grimsdale laughed.

"But doesn't the forestry commission slap a ban on shooting wildfowl if they're *driven* by weather to the south?" He knew he shouldn't have said it; he was usually more controlled. When he looked at this rosy-cheeked, iron-haired, smug Master of Foxhounds and Harriers, he couldn't help himself. The look on Grimsdale's face, as if he'd lost an old poaching-partner, told Melrose he'd have to make up the points if he wanted information.

"That's quite a stag there, Mr. Grimsdale." Melrose raised his eyes to the twelve-pointer, the one Grimsdale himself had been admiring. "Where'd you get that one?"

"Auchnacraig. That's in Scotland."

"I've heard of it," said Melrose, without the trace of a smile. Nice to get the geography lesson along with how to shoot just about anything that walked or flew. But Grimsdale was bathing so much in his own glow, he didn't notice.

"Ah yes. Twenty-one stone. Nearly got a silver on that one."

Melrose assumed he meant a medal. He smiled bleakly. "Wonderful. Where do you hunt the stag around these parts, Mr. Grimsdale?"

"Exmoor. For your red deer, that's the place. For buck, the New Forest. Donaldson's one of the best harborers there is. He's the one out at first light to find a warrantable stag. Can't get on without a shrewd harborer."

"Right. Just as the superintendent can't go without his sergeant."

For some reason, Grimsdale thought this rather rich and slapped his arm around Melrose's shoulders. Given the multiple brandies he'd had that evening, the ruddy glow of his complexion could have competed with the rather remarkable sunset they'd seen a few hours before.

"What did you think of Sally MacBride?" asked Melrose, suddenly.

The arm dropped just as suddenly away. "The MacBride woman?" The irritation gave way to feigned remorse. "Incredible thing, the way she died." He shook his head, drank his brandy, gazed up at a broad beam of antlers, and repeated it. He might have been talking about the stag.

Melrose was sick of this dismissal of the death of the woman. "What do you make of the dogs and the cat?"

"Cat? Dogs?" he said, as if he'd never heard of anything that didn't run with a pack. "Oh, you mean, the Quick woman's dog. And the others? Well, what about it?" He answered his own question about Gerald Jenks's dog. "Good riddance. Tore up my damned rosebushes." The glow deepened to the ruddier flush of anger.

"How well did you know them — Una Quick and Sally MacBride, I mean?"

Grimsdale was still looking at the stag, smiling. What was the life of the odd villager or two compared with twelve points and twenty stone? Then he refilled his glass and offered Melrose another. Melrose shook his head, wondering if the man were stalling, or merely dreaming of Auchnacraig and Exmoor. If dreaming, he seemed to waken suddenly to the distinct oddity of Lord Ardry's questions.

"I don't understand. I knew Miss Quick — she was postmistress, after all, everyone knew her. And Mrs. MacBride. I go to the Deer Leap, don't I? Only pub in the village, unfortunately." He looked about at his own superior accommodations smugly. "They'd — he'd do better to fix it up a bit. But of course, *she* was such a layabout —"

Grimsdale stopped, coughed. Whether he saw the unintended pun, or simply thought it rude to speak ill of the dead, Melrose didn't know. But he did know the conversation would stalk all over hunt country if Melrose didn't get his eye off that hare Grimsdale was now hefting in his hand. "What would you say to these women having been murdered, Mr. Grimsdale?"

The stuffed hare was replaced with a thud. *"What?"* Grimsdale looked slightly wild and then he laughed. It was a hearty laugh. *"Murdered?* Murder in Ashdown Dean?"

"It could,"said Melrose mildly, "happen anywhere."

"Not here," said Grimsdale, his eye now caught by a gray fox.

"Why do you think Scotland Yard is here, then? To investigate a case of cardiac arrest?"

"But that's what it was, man! If the damned fool woman didn't know enough not to go out in a storm up to that call box . . ." He shrugged.

"Her telephone wasn't working, apparently. Was yours?"

"Mine? Damned if I know. I wasn't making any calls around that time."

"What time?"

Grimsdale stopped his inspection of the hare, looked sharply at Melrose, and said smugly, "You're asking questions like police, sir. But you can't catch me out with that old ruse. *Everyone* heard about Una Quick falling out of that call box close on ten. After all, one of my guests was the person she fell across. Praed, her name is. But you know her. Has some monster of a cat that's clawed up half the draperies in her room. See she pays for 'em, there'll be no mistake. Have to get a decorator in. Or get Amanda Crowley to sew a new batch."

He stood there, apparently dreaming away about how he could stick Polly for the price of the drapes, while getting Amanda to volunteer her talents as seamstress.

Melrose lit up another cigar, trying to think how best to lie to get at the truth. "Ridiculous, of course, but you're probably aware there's been some talk in Ashdown about you and Mrs. MacBride."

Grimsdale's face seemed to take on all the hues of the fire in the grate. Eyes electric blue and sparking, cheeks like licks of flame, iron hair like volcanic ash. *"That is a lie!* What in God's name would I be doing with the likes of that common . . . Anyway, Amanda and I —" He stopped short on that one, and quickly asked, "Where'd you hear it?"

"Here and there. She was known to take that little river walk at night that ends up, I suppose, at your pond. With the tame mallard." Melrose smiled briefly.

Sebastian Grimsdale collapsed in a chair, and Melrose thought some confession was forthcoming. Then he sat up. "If you must know, there's been talk about the MacBride woman and my kennel master. Thought Donaldson was smarter than that. I'd see a light in the stable house. Wondered what he'd be doing up at that hour. I let him live in that place just back of the kennels."

Having reached his own solution to his satisfaction, Grimsdale sat back and lit up a cigar, shaking and shaking his head. "There it is, then. Fancy."

"I imagine the superintendent might want to have a talk with him, then."

"Can't imagine *why*. Donaldson's from Scotland. Got nothing to do with these people. He's just here for the season."

Melrose laughed, "Well, one can get up to any number of things waiting —"

He was interrupted by one of the most terrible rackets he'd ever heard.

"My God! *What's that?*" Grimsdale shot out of his chair and looked wildly at Melrose. "Sounds like hounds rioting."

It did indeed. Before Melrose could put down his glass and chuck his cigar into the fireplace, Grimsdale had rushed from the trophy room through the french windows and out into the court.

Melrose followed in the direction of the kennels and stableyard, where a soupy fog closed around him. In the midst of the chorus of foxhounds came the eerie sound of the deep baying of Grimsdale's staghounds.

And as Melrose tried to make his way through the fog, he thought that mixed with all of this riot was the sound of a scream that no hound would make.

The handsome Donaldson was handsome no longer. He lay inside the kennel, ravaged by the staghounds, one of which lay beside him. In the light of Grimsdale's torch, Melrose saw the other hound stagger and fall, its light markings now blood-smeared.

Then he heard feet running across the courtyard. Wiggins. Polly.

Grimsdale, having stood frozen, looking down at the bloody kennel floor, suddenly shouted, *"Get Fleming!"*

And that, thought Melrose, turning to stop Polly in her tracks, pretty well spoke the man's obsession. Call for the vet, not the physician. Though Farnsworth couldn't have done Donaldson any good now, neither could Fleming help the staghounds.

Wiggins took the torch from Grimsdale's hand as Melrose practically had to wrestle with Polly to keep her away. "Nothing for you to see, old girl —"

"Oh, shut up." She broke from his grasp, peered through the fog along the tracery of torchlight, and was back in an instant. "For once, you're right." Polly buried her head against his shoulder.

Across her dark head, Melrose squinted. A form seemed to emerge from the mist at the other end of the stableyard. It seemed to undulate as it came toward them, became a ghostly blob, finally turned into a recognizable form. Carrie Fleet.

A very dirty-looking Carrie Fleet.

When Grimsdale saw her, he stared for a few seconds and then slowly raised the rifle.

Melrose disengaged himself from Polly, but Wiggins, fortunately, was quicker. With a judolike kick, he knocked Grimsdale's rifle arm upward and the shot went wide, broke glass somewhere — possibly one of the stable house windows.

Calmly, Wiggins took the gun. "I think that'll be enough, sir. I really think that'll be quite enough."

Carrie Fleet just stood there, motionless.

Grimsdale screamed. *"You devil! Always trouble —"*

Melrose clamped his hand around Grimsdale's arm. If anyone were possessed, he thought, it was Grimsdale.

"What're you doing here, Carrie?" whispered Polly.

Carrie Fleet jerked her thumb over her shoulder toward the edge of the New Forest. "Unstopping earths. I heard hounds." She walked over to the kennels and peered in at the body of Donaldson and the dead hounds.

She shook her head and shook it. Then she looked one by one into the several cages housing the beagles.

Then she turned and walked back into the fog that closed round her like a glove.

No one tried to stop her. The night was deathly quiet.

"There's no way of knowing for sure until I do an autopsy —"

Grimsdale, a large balloon-glass of brandy in hands that might have been palsied with all of their shaking, said, "They'd never have turned on Donaldson. Never."

"We seem to have evidence to the contrary," said Melrose coldly.

Wiggins, in the absence of Jury, wanted to get down to business. "Dr. Fleming — ?"

"I was about to say. It could be one of several drugs, administered anytime from minutes to days or even weeks before. Something like fentanyl. But that's not easy to come by — unless you're a doctor or a vet. Then there's benzodiazafine. Valium. Easy enough to get hold of." Fleming shrugged. "I'd have to do an autopsy."

Wiggins made a note of that and said, with a frown, "That would mean that *whoever* went into that kennel would have been torn apart."

"Yes," said Fleming.

"But there were only two people who did," said Melrose. "And Mr. Grimsdale, here, wouldn't have gone into the kennel for any particular reason, not until tomorrow."

Polly Praed, sitting in the trophy room in her old brown wrapper, chewed at her lip. "And that's the third one. The murderer could have been anywhere when it happened. What a bloody awful way to kill a man."

Melrose's thoughts were on Polly Praed's head on his shoulder when she added, turning those amethyst eyes on Wiggins. "But aren't you going to get Superintendent Jury back here at the double?"

Twenty-seven

"**A**nd where do you think *you're* going?" asked Polly Praed the next morning. She had just walked into the Lodge's breakfast room to see Melrose finishing a sumptuous — by Gun Lodge standards — breakfast. The piece of toast she plucked from the toast rack was actually warm. So was the piece of bacon she plucked from his plate. "It's only just gone nine."

Then, apparently having lost interest in Melrose's designs, she looked around the room. "I should have thought he'd be here by now."

He meaning Jury. Melrose sighed. "According to Wiggins, the superintendent had rather a full schedule yesterday. But he might come walking in at any minute, so I suggest you get dressed. Not that the robe is unbecoming; I'm sure Sherlock Holmes would have loved it. Sorry I ate my breakfast," he added, seeing her staring at his plate. "But I imagine the Grimsdale cook, unobstructed by Grimsdale, will provide you with one."

"Where is the awful man?"

"In the trophy room, last I saw. With Pasco and Detective Inspector Russell. Grimsdale does not look at all well."

"He shouldn't. He should look like death. He was going to *kill* that child. If it hadn't been for Sergeant Wiggins . . . Where *are* you going?"

"To 'La Notre.' "

"At this hour? Don't baronesses and so forth sleep until noon?"

"I have no idea. But she might rise to see the Earl of Caverness."

"Impostor," said Polly, chewing the last piece of toast.

ⅺ

To see her, however, one ran the gamut.

Melrose's Silver Ghost probably hastened the running of it, he guessed. A little maid in a cockeyed cap stared at it and then at him and the card he handed her, uncertain as to which of the three was the most impressive.

"I don't mean to bother the Baroness Regina at this rather ungodly hour —" Melrose smiled. "I thought perhaps I could see —"

"Oh, I'm sure it's no bother, Your Grace —"

He laughed. "I haven't reached those heady heights. Only an earl."

"Hullo," said a voice from the shadows of the foyer. "Gillian Kendall." Gillian put out her hand. "Regina's secretary."

"Miss Kendall." She had been sorting the post on a silver plate, rather tarnished. "Sorry to be dropping by so early." If nearly ten could be so considered.

She replaced the post and said, "That business last night at the Lodge. That was absolutely dreadful. . . ."

"Carrie told you?"

Gillian Kendall looked puzzled. "Carrie? No. What did she have to do with it?" Then she smiled. "Though she does have a way of turning up when there's an animal crisis."

It was Melrose who was puzzled now. "I'd call it more of a Carrie crisis. She didn't tell you —?"

Before he could finish the statement, a vision, if not precisely of loveliness, but a vision nonetheless, came sweeping down the staircase. "How very kind of you to call, Lord Ardry. Coffee in the salon, Gillian?"

"Yes, of course. But what about Carrie?"

"Carrie? Carrie?" said the Baroness, attempting to up-sweep her hair and hold it with the hairpins in her mouth. The mouth had been rather quickly painted; lipstick bleeding into the tiny pursed lines around it. Regina de la Notre apparently had no compunction about completing her toilette in public. "Carrie is always in trouble." She sighed and stopped with her hair-pinning. "*Now* what's she done? And to a peer of the realm, dear God."

"It's more what's been done to Carrie."

"Well, dear God! Why are we all standing here?" She said it as if chairs should materialize out of the very air, and looked sharply at Gillian, as if her magic act were rotten.

Gillian opened the doors into the salon and Regina swept in. Her dressing gown was definitely the sweeping sort, blue brocade and ivory insets and a long train.

Having arranged herself on a chaise longue and accepted a light for her cigarette, she was ready for the day's disasters. Gillian still stood. "Now, what is all this?"

"Grimsdale nearly killed her last night. If it hadn't been for Sergeant Wiggins, I doubt she'd be alive — I can't imagine her not telling you."

Both of them looked horrified, Regina enough that she seemed pulled from her chaise by invisible wires. She started pacing. "Blast and damn that man." She whirled with quite an exquisite movement of pulling the train of brocade with her hand. "I trust the police have got him."

"Questioned him, yes. Got him —?" Melrose shrugged.

"Assault with a deadly weapon — Gillian, will you please not stand there like a stick, dammit. Coffee!"

"Don't you think Carrie takes precedence over coffee?" Gillian said, icily.

Fortunately the little maid was back, given instructions, and Gillian went out through the french doors. Despite the greater concerns of the morning, Melrose could not help but be fascinated by the *trompe l'oeil* murals.

When the Baroness had stopped her pacing, and restored herself to the chaise and another cigarette, Melrose told her what had happened.

"*Donaldson?* Killed by those beasts of Grimsdale's?" She shuddered. Then she turned to Melrose. "I've been visited by a Scotland Yard superintendent. What on earth is your particular interest in all of this?" She plucked up his card from the table beside the chaise. "Earl of Caverness."

Melrose smiled. "More or less."

"I beg your pardon?"

"My name is really Melrose Plant."

"Mine's Gigi Scroop. From Liverpool. I am actually a *real* baroness, not that it gets me much but lording it over the village. Why do you pass yourself off as an earl, then?"

"It's not quite that. I simply gave up my titles."

A well-plucked eyebrow shot up. "I'll be damned. *Gave* them up? Well, to each his own tastes. Now, Grimsdale is done for, I hope. That should get him five to ten, wouldn't you say?"

"Possibly —"

Gillian was back. "She's with her menagerie. Not talking. It doesn't surprise me. Bingo — that's her dog — is missing."

"Then I can imagine she'd be worried."

He stood up. "Mind if I have a word with her?"

"Of course you may," Regina swept her arm toward the french door. "It's her sanctuary. Displaced-animal thing. I

don't mind, if that's what keeps her happy. I only wish she'd
get rid of the damned rooster. I'm not Judas."

"No coffee, Mr. Plant?" asked Gillian.

"Later, thank you."

As he started for the door, she said. "You're a friend of the
superintendent?"

Melrose turned. "Yes."

She colored slightly. "You wouldn't know when —"

"He's coming back?" He smiled wearily. "Sometime
today." Certainly, she was a good-looking woman.

Not that that would get *him* anywhere.

⋊

She was taking a black cat out of a makeshift cage when he
stood at the door to the little house. Or "Sanctuary," he supposed, looking up at the rough-cut sign above the door.

Given the cat, an elderly Labrador, two badgers, a rooster,
and what he could have sworn was a pony that had peered at
him out of the trees, Melrose had to admit that Carrie Fleet
didn't play favorites. It didn't even have to walk on all fours,
apparently, given the rooster clawing at the dirt floor with its
bandaged leg.

None of the animals seemed in terribly good repair — the
Labrador looked as if it had been hit by a lorry. It lay quietly
in a wooden box with slats, eyes blinking, breathing slowly.

"Oh. Hullo," said Carrie, in the act of putting a much-
abused stuffed mouse at the other end of the room. Hut
would have been an apter description than "Sanctuary."

"Hello, there." He waited, with a warm smile, supposing
her own greeting, not awfully friendly, but certainly not cold,
to be the forerunner to a lengthy conversation about animal
welfare.

It wasn't. She had squatted down to give the cat a small
push, apparently trying to work up interest in the mouse.

There was something wrong with one of its hind legs, and it seemed resistant. "Go on, then," said Carrie, giving it another little push.

"Well. I suppose it needs a bit of exercise, that it?"

She nodded.

It was as if the events of last night hadn't happened. She just crouched there, running her long silvery hair behind her ear, watching the cat. Eventually, it got interested and made its clever play for the mouse.

She got up then, looking relieved.

"You have a way with animals, certainly. . . ." And then he felt an absolute fool as she looked at him with those milky-blue eyes almost devoid of expression.

"If you call not hitting them with cars and sticks."

Almost a whole sentence. He wondered what it would take to get a smile out of her.

"Generally, of course, I don't bother about the drover and his sheep. Just plow the car right through them." Melrose's own smile was brilliant.

It went unanswered.

He coughed. "Look, couldn't I talk with you for a minute?"

"You are." She opened the cage where the dog lay, ran her hand down its back, not so much petting it, but more in the manner of a doctor whose fingers can feel what the eye can't see nor the ear hear.

Damn. Melrose would have hated to report to Jury he couldn't get the girl to talk. "I'm a friend of the superintendent —"

That should get a reaction. And the usual question.

"Is he coming back?" There was a hesitancy, though, as if asking it gave something away.

"Of course. Today, I'm sure."

"Then maybe he can find Bingo."

"Bingo — oh. Your dog. I'm dreadfully sorry he's missing."

She came to the door of the dark little hut, blinking in the morning light. "At least you didn't say, 'He'll turn up.' "

Had Melrose's long-standing habit of refusing cheap condolences actually done him some good? "Don't you think he will?"

Carrie squinted off toward the horizon and was silent, as if her eye scanned the hill for some sign of Bingo. She was perfectly still, fingering a narrow gold chain around her neck.

There was a bench there and Melrose sat down. "Would you mind sitting?"

She shrugged. Standing, sitting — little difference.

"Sebastian Grimsdale's in a good deal of trouble about last night. I can't imagine a man being so obsessed —" There had been very few times in his life when Melrose blushed. This was one.

But all he caught was a flicker of a smile. "He's awful. With him, it's either a huntable buck or trash." She leaned over, her elbows resting on her knees.

"I had rather a long lecture on the intricacies of stag-hunting."

" 'Nasty beasts,' he calls them. Probably didn't say anything about what deer do to escape. Like jump over cliffs. Try to swim out to sea —"

If Melrose thought he'd got a long lecture from Grimsdale, it was nothing to what he was getting from Carrie Fleet. Silent on other matters, she was extremely voluble on the subject of animals. It ended, the list of deer-hunting atrocities, with the story of a buck that had fallen under a van and got pulled out by its antlers and its throat slashed in full view of the villagers.

"And he bags foxes," she went on, staring straight ahead.

He was taken with her magnificent profile. Who had been this girl's forebears?

". . . see the one there?"

Melrose shook his head to clear it.

"I'm sorry. The what?"

"Fox. He keeps it in a kennel. He'll let it go and set hounds on it. That's what he does, and it's against the rules. I've read the rules."

Melrose could believe she'd *written* them.

"What he does is, if a fox goes to ground and he can't get a badger or terrier to get it out, he does it with tools and has a bag. That's how he got the one he has now." Carrie looked at Melrose, her pale blue eyes like glistening ice. "When a fox goes to ground and finds a rabbit hole or something, that's supposed to be sanctuary." Suddenly, she got up. "I've got to look for Bingo."

"Carrie, just a second. Pasco will be round, of course. You'll be asked to press charges." She seemed not to comprehend. "You know. Against Grimsdale."

"Why? Because he almost shot me?" She shrugged, still scanning the horizon. "He'd have missed, anyway."

Not at that range. "Are you saying you're not *going* to? It was assault with a deadly weapon."

"Someone killed his dogs. I guess I'd get pretty upset too."

Melrose couldn't believe it. "But you *loathe* the man!"

Her face was again without expression. "He's not warrantable. He's trash." She started to walk off and turned again. "When Mr. Jury comes back . . ."

The sentence hovered there, unfinished.

⊠

Jury was, at that moment, sitting in his flat, smoking, turning over pages of reports he had accumulated from various branches of New Scotland Yard. They told him next to nothing. Brindle had been nicked once for extortion that hardly seemed worth the trouble. Probably he had tried it on several times, maybe got away with it, maybe not. It seemed to be the way he spent his leisure time when he wasn't watching the telly and drinking.

As for the Lister family, nil. What the old man had told him was confirmed by the odd newspaper report — about the Listers, not about Carrie Fleet. Or Carolyn, assuming they were one and the same. They had to be — there wasn't a break in the chain of events that had led up to that accidental meeting with Regina —

Jury shook another cigarette out of the packet that lay on the arm of the chair. A family far flung, the Listers. Son, daughter, a couple of cousins. And a sister. He had mentioned a sister near his own age.

The match burnt Jury's finger as he thought about Gigi Scroop from Liverpool. He took Brindle's letter out again. ". . . well, Floss and me thought, having the care of her all them —" And the *them* crossed out, *these* printed in above it. Extortionists have to be careful of their grammar; Jury couldn't help but smiling over this. "— years, that this ought to call for just a bit more, don't you think, Baroness?" Probably the title had been suggested by Flossie. Add a touch of class, even though she'd already forgotten what the class was.

Jury dropped the letter atop the other papers and frowned. If Una Quick had taken the picture, she might have had blackmail in mind. But how could she put this particular two and two together? "Amy Lister" would have, in Una's mind, no association with Carrie Fleet.

But in somebody else's mind?

Someone in Ashdown Dean was smart enough to put Carrie Fleet into that picture and see there was money in it —

He was shaken from this brown study by a knock at the door.

Carole-anne stood there, dressed again as only Carole-anne could, meaning she looked undressed. Skintight leathers she was wearing today and a parrot green T-shirt. And behind her, clutching her black handbag to her black bosom, Mrs. Wasserman, all smiles.

Carole-anne draped herself in Jury's doorway, all smiles

herself. "Took your gear back, Super. I mean, can you see me in sable?" From her ears dripped long, bluish-green bits of glass, like tears. "Mrs W. and me" — she nodded at Mrs. W., behind her — "we're going down the pub. *Come* on, then."

Jury stared, blinked, stared like a man who'd just had the bandages taken from his eyes. "Mrs. *Wasserman?*"

"It's more fun you need to have, Superintendent. We were just saying that maybe we could get you out."

Carole-anne smiled her syrupy little smile and winked slowly. "Don't be such an old stick, Super. Down the Angel for an hour and you'll look near human."

"Down the Angel for an hour and you'll have to carry me back. I've got to —"

Carole-anne rolled her heavenly eyes toward heaven. "Oh, God. You've *always* got to." She was pulling on his sleeve. "We need an escort, right, Mrs. W.?"

"Absolutely, Mr. Jury. You would not want unattended women going to the pub." She slid a glance toward Carole-anne and winked at Jury.

"See. Outvoted." Carole-anne lounged and chewed her gum.

Jury laughed. "Half an hour."

"Oh, hell, how wonderful. *Vous serez toujours dans mon souvenir.*"

Mrs. Wasserman was clicking the clasp on her purse open and shut, nervously. "This one, she has an ear, a real *ear* for languages. I tell her if she studied, the Common Market would hire her as a translator."

Carole-anne plucked at her teardrop earrings. "Just what I always wanted."

Twenty-eight

The note was delivered on the silver salver, along with the rest of the post.

Carrie, sitting at the luncheon table, had been staring blindly at her salad, thinking about Bingo. She hadn't seen him since last night, when she'd been out unstopping earths.

"He'll turn up, Carrie," said Gillian, but without much conviction in her tone.

"Like the others?" Her face, her tone were void of expression.

Gillian handed the Baroness the post, and said, "Animals *do* wander off, Carrie —"

"How would you know?" There was no inflection, no bitterness in the tone; it seemed only a mild question.

It was true; neither Gillian nor Regina had shown interest in the sanctuary: the infrequent visits they made to it were born of curiosity, nothing more.

The Baroness, at least, had the sense not to offer cheap comfort. Or perhaps she was simply more interested in her letters. As she smoked and drank her coffee, Gillian read two of them to Regina. Then she frowned and handed Carrie a small envelope. "It's for you."

Carrie, who never got any letters, was as surprised as were Gillian and Regina. It had been posted in Selby. Carrie wondered who in Selby would be writing to her — Neahle, perhaps? Maxine might have broken down and taken her on market day. The scrawl was childish, large loops of letters. But why would Neahle —?

"Aren't you going to open it, for heaven's sake? It might be some news."

Regina sounded really concerned.

Bingo. It was not a word; it was a small picture of a bingo board. The entire note consisted of pictures. Cut from a book or magazine, more likely a child's playbook, was one of those maze-puzzles. Then — and here Carrie's iron control nearly broke — a snapshot of the Rumford Laboratory. Taken at night. Floodlit on that empty field, it looked all the more like a prison.

That was all. Carrie stared past Gillian, who looked at her anxiously, as Regina asked, "Well, what *is* it?"

Carrie was about to say something and then stopped. For she knew, she knew with the swiftness of Limerick taking to the air, and with the surety of a lock clicking closed on a cage, that whatever this was, it wasn't some silly game Neahle was playing. That whoever had done it, with the exception of the address, was being incredibly careful not to give away the sender's identity. It was a warning. Or a direction . . . ?

Regina had just jogged her arm impatiently. "Carrie?"

Carrie shrugged and said calmly, "Oh, it's just some silly pictures Neahle sent me."

"Neahle? Good grief, I didn't even know she could write."

Carrie had pocketed the envelope and paper. "Maybe she

got Maxine to do it. Maybe just to cheer me up. May I be excused?"

"I don't know why you bother to ask. I'd have to chain you to a chair to keep you from doing what you want to."

"I guess," said Carrie, pushing back her chair.

Not until she was out in the sanctuary did she take the paper out again. Almost absently, she fed the animals — misfeeding the Labrador, who let out a whine. No wonder, she thought. She'd given him chickenfeed. *Keep your head,* she told herself. *Keep your head or Bingo's going to die.* She let Blackstone out and gave him his food and the mouse. Her jobs done, she sat down to study the threat.

Through the opening of the old folly she looked at the maze. Why? Why would someone want her to go into the maze? She knew every inch of it. Carrie looked back at the picture. What she thought had been meant as the "La Notre" maze was not that — this one was square, the sort of thing scientists run rats and mice through with some kind of reward at the end.

So it was merely another pointer to the lab. And when she had been there those weeks ago, the demonstrators, several of them, had been taking pictures by torchlight.

All right. Carrie sat on her stool, perfectly still. Someone either had or was going to take Bingo to the lab.

The only person she knew of who had access to it was Paul Fleming. She frowned. She didn't like him much, really, because of his work, but what on earth would he want with Bingo? Why would anyone want to hurt Bingo?

Sebastian Grimsdale. For revenge, maybe. But would he have poisoned the Potter sisters' cat and killed the two dogs? Carrie frowned. Una Quick had died and Sally MacBride. But nothing had happened to the Potters or Gerald Jenks. She saw no connection.

It didn't make sense. She had the funny feeling that what she held in her hands now was all she was going to get. This person wasn't going to chance another note, and was depending on her to be smart enough to figure out what she had right there.

What she was supposed to do was go to the Rumford Lab, at night. No way to tell which night. So she'd have to go every night until she knew what was going on.

ɔ

Sebastian Grimsdale, although still showing the effects of the previous night, was coming round to his old self. His chief concern appeared to be that what had happened had resulted in there being no meet.

Jury had got back to Ashdown Dean to find Wiggins dredging up totally unnecessary apologies for not having got hold of him sooner. Plant had credited Wiggins with saving Carrie Fleet's life. Hardly a need for apologies, Jury assured him.

"If anyone's to blame, I am. That you couldn't reach me. Where's Grimsdale?" he'd asked as the three of them had stood in the large foyer of Gun Lodge, overseen by several racks of antlers.

Between Grimsdale and Amanda Crowley, it might have been a wake. Amanda was dressed in her usual breeches, stock perfectly done up. Her tweed jacket was slung over the arm of the chair. Grimsdale had had plenty of brandy and was in the act of telling her to stay to dinner when Jury and the others walked in.

"I don't think Mrs. Crowley will have time for that," said Jury.

As they stared at this bizarre infringement upon their freedom, Jury looked at Amanda Crowley. In that gear, eyes the color of dry sherry. Lips, although touched up, equally dry. "Sergeant Wiggins would like a word with her."

Since Wiggins wasn't sure what word he'd like, Jury tore a page from his notebook and handed it to the sergeant.

Grimsdale sputtered. Jury overrode whatever objection he was going to make. "And I'd like to hear your story, Mr. Grimsdale."

Amanda remained seated. "I've no idea what this means."

"You will," said Jury in a voice that lifted her from her chair. Then, escorted by Sergeant Wiggins, who, ever the gentleman, offered her a throat lozenge, she marched from the room.

"I'm sick of being dogged by police." He reddened at his own pun.

"That's too bad. I'd like to hear your story," Jury repeated, sitting and helping himself to the cigarette box on the table.

"I've told it often enough —"

"I'd like to hear it, Mr. Grimsdale."

Grimsdale reluctantly told him what had happened the night before, piecemeal. Of course he hadn't aimed the rifle at the child. Although he was quite sure she had something to do with it —

"Carrie Fleet? Probably the only person who wouldn't."

"She despises me, despises hunting — the whole lot."

"Please be logical. It's just for that reason she *wouldn't* have harmed those staghounds. But it is very likely you *would* have harmed her."

Trying to drag a red herring across the path, Grimsdale said, "And it's *illegal*, Superintendent, to go about unstopping earths!"

He took a pull at his brandy.

"What was Mrs. Crowley's relationship with your keeper? Donaldson?"

"I beg your pardon?"

Impatiently, Jury shook his head. "You know what I mean."

"I know what you *mean*, and I resent it."

"Unfortunately, resentment means sod-all to me." He smiled.

"There was no . . . *relationship*. Good lord, man, everyone knew Donaldson and —" He stopped.

" 'And.' Go on." Jury smiled inwardly. Plant had used the same trick.

Jury merely wanted to confirm the rumor.

"It would be ungentlemanly of me."

"That's a shame. Be ungentlemanly. Your keeper and Sally MacBride were having an affair, that it?"

"That was the rumor. I pay no attention to rumors."

Jury bet. "Whose time do you want to waste, Mr. Grimsdale? Mine or the Hampshire C.I.D.'s?"

Grimsdale waved him back into his chair. "Oh, all right, all right. He had his separate digs in the stable house. That's where they met."

"Cozy. Anywhere else?"

"How should I know? Listen, you've no right to browbeat —"

"I'm not. But I could. You tried to kill a fifteen-year-old girl."

Grimsdale shot up. "*And were you there, Superintendent?*"

"No. With three witnesses, I hardly needed to be, did I? Now, tell me if you're familiar with the name Lister."

In the act of lighting a cigarette, Jury nearly dropped the match when Grimsdale said, "Of course."

"What?"

Moving impatiently in his chair, Grimsdale said, "Can't imagine why you'd be interested. You know the way we name hounds. Use one letter a lot of the time. Lister's one of them. Then there's Laura, Lawrence, Luster —"

"I see. I was thinking of a *person*. A Lord Lister."

"Person? Oh. No, I never heard the name."

"Tell me about Amanda Crowley, then."

"What about her?" His tone was convincingly indifferent. "Been living in Ashdown ten, maybe a dozen years. I don't keep *count*."

Jury watched his eye travel from stag's head to buck's to birds under glass. He certainly did, of some things. "She has money of her own?"

"I don't know."

"She doesn't seem to do any work, Mr. Grimsdale. One would assume she has money of her own. An allowance? A trust fund? Something like that?"

Grimsdale leaned forward, brandy glass clutched between his hands. "Are you suggesting I'm a fortune-hunter?"

Jury smiled. "Why not? You hunt everything else."

"Nothing, sir." Wiggins flipped through his notes. "She was here this morning because the hunt didn't meet at the Deer Leap, and she rode over to find out what was happening. Been here ever since."

"How convivial. Breakfast, lunch, and a supper we interrupted."

"Yes, sir. But given the food in *this* place . . ." Wiggins shuddered. "Never had such stiffish oatmeal, sir, and then —"

"Too bad, Wiggins. The name Lister —?"

The sergeant shook his head. "Claimed it meant nothing to her. Never heard it before." Wiggins folded the bit of paper and slid a lozenge into his mouth. "Believe me, I watched her responses sharp as a cat."

"Unfortunately, people can be sharp as cats too. But not to worry. I didn't expect much." He paused. "In my next report, you can bet what you did last night will be detailed."

Seldom did Sergeant Wiggins laugh aloud. Now he did. " 'Next report,' sir? Do you ever make them?"

"Intermittently. Where're Polly and Plant?"

'At the Deer Leap, for some food. I expect even Maxine could put something together better than what you get here.

As long as she doesn't have to cook it," he added glumly, and then sighed. "Poor Miss Praed." Seeing Jury putting on his coat, Wiggins pulled his scarf about his neck.

"Why 'poor'?"

"Got all scratched up. Trying to get that hulk she calls a cat from running up the Lodge's draperies."

"Hope he did a good job. On the draperies, not on Polly. She should take a lesson from Carrie Fleet."

As they let themselves out into the cold dusk, Wiggins said, "That reminds me. Mr. Plant wanted me to tell you. The girl Carrie's dog. It's missing."

"Bingo?"

"Yes, sir. She wanted, Mr. Plant thought, to see you. Though she didn't say it directly."

"She wouldn't."

Twenty-nine

amn the man! Revenge! You can bet on it!" Regina de
la Notre had dropped her languid air and paced
about the salon trailing behind her a vermilion coat of
Chinese silk and in one hand a bottle of gin, which she used
to top up her glass. She had been pacing now for a good ten
minutes — back and forth, back and forth, mural to mural —
and Jury wondered whether her turns at each wall and the
passing of herself in front of the huge mirror might not have
been done as much for effect as angry tirade. The bottle of
gin didn't quite fit that image.

She went on ranting. Wiggins, notebook out and handkerchief on the little Sheraton table, looked gratefully at his
cuppa and unhappily at the gin. They had been there nearly
an hour and the bottle had been in more or less constant motion. *Cocktail hour,* she had said when they walked in, inviting one and all to join. Where was Lord Ardry? Charming
man. Jury thought he and Miss Praed had gone to the Deer
Leap for a meal. How utterly revolting, and who is Miss
Praed?

To Jury's questions about Woburn Place it was no, no, no.

No, she had never heard the name Lister; no, she knew nothing about any sort of Alsatian; no, she had never seen Carrie before the meeting at the Silver Vaults, and what in *hell* were all of these questions about? She seemed to blame not Jury, who was asking them, but Wiggins, who was writing down the answers.

All of this was taking place amidst pacing and sweepings of silk with her hand, and interspersed with the continued harangue. "*Grimsdale* — that odious creature — has done something to that terrier of hers, what does she call it?" The Baroness snapped her fingers as if in a fit of forgetfulness and addressed this question to Gillian.

"Bingo."

Jury thought the look Gillian gave her employer was close to loathing. As if she thought the Baroness might, after all this time, at least remember the name of Carrie's dog. Which, Jury was pretty sure, Regina did. She merely strived for effects.

As now she clutched her fists to her handsome silk coat (one fist still around the neck of the bottle) and exclaimed: "He could actually believe Carrie — *Carrie* — had a hand in those damned dogs of his being poisoned? The creature's round the twist, ought to be put away." Distractedly, she looked about her like a woman gone quite mad with the news (which Jury was sure she hadn't; it merely made a change) and asked, "Where's Carrie? Where is she?"

"Looking for Bingo, of course. Or in her animal hut, brooding. What would you expect?" said Gillian. She was now standing in front of the mirror, thus blocking Regina's view of herself. Between the twin doors, the twin *trompe l'oeil* murals which again doubled the doors and the view outside, and the mirror facing the mirror on the back wall, Jury felt he had fallen, perhaps like Alice, into a world of reflections.

Regina, by now quite drunk, though carrying it off to a fare-thee-well, ran her hand in a tragic gesture across her forehead. "She must be back for dinner. She knows we dine at eight-thirty."

Gillian raised her eyes to heaven and shook her head. Her dress tonight was a grayish brown, different from the other only in its style. Had she been asked to play down her own looks in order to enhance Regina's, she couldn't have done a better job. But colorless as the dress was, it was draped across breast and hip in such a way that — like the other — it could hardly hide what lay beneath.

"So your meeting with Carrie Fleet was accidental," said Jury mildly. The Silver Vaults were famous, well visited. It was possible that anyone in London might have gone there. No particular reason to be suspicious, but all the same . . . Liverpool could not be accounted for in the accent and aristocratic cheekbones of Regina de la Notre.

The Baroness stopped in her tracks and came to look down at him as if he, too, like Grimsdale, must be insane. "I *beg* your pardon? Accidental?" She bent slightly over Jury, who could have filled a shot glass from her breath alone. "Of course not, Superintendent. I traveled from Woburn Place to Eastcheap to Shoreditch to Blackheath to Threadneedle Street to the Old Curiosity Shop to the Silver Vaults. Just *searching*, my dear, for a thirteen-year-old animal-minder. *Good* God!" And she was back to pacing again.

Gillian was trying to look everywhere in the room but at Jury. "Your friend —" and now she paused for a name.

"Lord Ardry," said Jury, easily.

"Lord Ardry, yes. He was talking with Carrie this morning." She looked down at her intertwined hands. "I wonder if she told him about the note."

"What note was that?" Jury shifted uneasily, drank his whiskey.

"It came with the morning post. She said it was just some silly thing from Neahle Meara. I wondered about it; Carrie never gets letters."

"Never? No one in her past —" He turned to Regina. "Didn't you ever wonder, Baroness —"

"Regina," she corrected him, throatily, as she studied the mural before her.

"— about Carrie Fleet's past?"

"For God's sake, my dear, she hasn't a past."

Jury looked at her, bleakly. She was right.

Gillian ran through one of the french doors, calling over her shoulder she was going to look for Carrie.

As Jury got up to follow her, the little maid announced dinner.

"Well, my dear Sergeant, shall we . . . ?"

If there was any more to that question, Jury didn't hear it.

Gillian was standing at the door of the sanctuary, peering into blackness when Jury came up behind her.

"She's not *here*," Gillian wailed. It was hard to know if her face was wet with rain or tears. "She's *not here!*"

Jury put his arm round her and his hand on her satiny hair and held her. "Then she's looking for Bingo —"

"You don't understand, you don't understand, you don't —" And the weeping grew with every repetition. Jury drew her closer, as she kept shaking her head against his coat.

"Gillian. What was in that note? Why're you so upset?"

The silky head kept shaking back and forth, back and forth, like Regina's pacing. "I don't *know*. But something's wrong. Something's *wrong!* Carrie's so disciplined —" And she moved her head from Jury's shoulder to look up at him. "You don't know her. She really *likes* that old devil —"

It was obvious she meant Regina.

"Sorry. I didn't really mean that. But if dinner's at eight, Carrie's *there!*" She was breathing in great, sobbing breaths.

"I know . . . you don't . . . believe me. Jealousy . . . something . . . but oh, where *is* she?"

Jury pulled her back again, head against shoulder. "I'll find her. Right now, I want you to have some brandy and lie down. I'll take you up —"

She seemed not to hear him. He shook her. "Gillian. We can stroll through the maze. Then I'll take you up and tuck you in. Fair enough?"

He thought the bad joke might be lost in the wind and the rain, but she did smile a little. "Fair enough. But no stroll. I'm too done in."

As they walked away from the arbor, she kept stopping and looking back, so that he had to urge her toward the house.

ⅺ

After he saw that Gillian was in bed and drowsy from brandy and a sedative she'd taken from a small bottle, Jury went down the hall, looking for Carrie's room. It wasn't hard to distinguish it: snapshots of Bingo and other animals — possibly the ones at the Brindles', one with the Brindle daughter in it. Had they then been mates of a sort? Had it been, for all of her posture of indifference, a painful parting?

Jury sat on the narrow, white-counterpaned bed, in the narrow room, white-walled. No ruffles, no ribbons, no nonsense. He was sure the lack of ornament and the size of the room had nothing to do with Regina's pinching pennies. It was definitely a Carrie Fleet room.

He searched it. No note, no letter, but he hadn't really expected to find one; she was too smart to leave something important lying about, or hidden in a drawer. He opened the cupboard. The few garments hanging there — another sweater, another dress like the one she'd worn when he met her, a coat. He went through the pockets. From the pinafore he drew out a snapshot. A shot, taken at night of a building, nondescript looking, nothing he'd seen.

But no note. And he was sure the note had been important, otherwise she would have told them, at lunch, what was in it. Her dislike of talk Jury did not put down at all to secretiveness: he put it down to despair.

Despair. A feeling that would be disallowed by adults and turned into something like "just going through a stage." But Jury remembered sitting on a bed very similar to this one, only in a row of beds when he was a little younger than Carrie. For him, when his mother and father were killed in the Second World War, it had been an orphanage until an uncle had rescued him. For Carrie, it had been the Brindles, until the Baroness had rescued *her*.

If rescue it had been.

⊐

The scene in the dining room was a delight. The Baroness at one end of a long rosewood table, Wiggins at the other. They seemed to be getting on like a house on fire, a lively conversation in progress, probably owing more to the three wineglasses at each place than to Wiggins's verve and wit.

He could have asked Regina about the snapshot, but thought better of it.

"Sergeant," said Jury, interrupting.

"Sir!" Wiggins stood up, his napkin falling to the floor.

Jury sighed. It was one of those times when Jury was the drill sergeant.

"My *dear* Superintendent! Please join us. My cook is superior —"

"Thanks, but I'm not hungry. It's after nine, Regina. Aren't you concerned about Carrie?"

"She's still looking for Bingo." Regina sighed and put down her wineglass. "I'd hardly expect her to report for dinner spot on eight-thirty."

"If you're through, Sergeant —"

Leaving Regina sighing over Gillian's absence — and no one to talk to — Jury and Wiggins got into their coats and then into their car.

"Where're we going, sir?"

"The Deer Leap. To find Plant. And Neahle Meara."

Wiggins turned in surprise. "The little girl, sir?"

"The little girl, yes."

⊠

They sat around the table in the saloon bar, used for the odd serving of meals, since few were served.

"I don't know," said Neahle. "*I* didn't write anything."

Jury smiled. "Didn't think you did. But what do you make of it, Neahle?"

The brown eyes looked from the snapshot and back at Jury. She shrugged. "*I* don't know." Her voice was tearful.

"It's all right, Neahle. Never mind then. Go on to bed."

But she sat like a rock now, her small chin in her fists. "Where's Carrie?"

"And what," asked Melrose Plant, "makes you think something's happened to Carrie?"

She looked away, toward the fire that had burned down to sparkless ashes. "Because you're all here asking funny questions." Then she slipped from her chair. "*I'm* going to bed." She ran out of the room.

The snap was passed around and around again. "Pasco? Maybe he'd know."

"What makes you think it's someplace around here?" asked Polly. "Maybe it's near the East India Docks."

"What a vivid imagination, Polly. All of that ground — looks just like the Thames."

"Call Pasco, Wiggins."

Wiggins left.

Plant took the picture and reluctantly headed for the bar, where Maxine Torres was wetting her finger, preparatory to turning a page in her magazine. Sullenly, she looked at Plant. *"Again?"* Obviously, she was referring to his pint of Old Peculiar. Plant, the raving alcoholic.

"No, Maxine, not another pint. It is your gorgeous black eyes I am interested in." He brought the picture near the eyes. "Recognize?"

She shoved it back. "Am I blind?"

"Don't know. Do you recognize this place?"

"Yeah. It's that lab outside town. Outside Selby. Mile, two miles." She was not interested in the snap or in the question. Or in Plant, certainly. Not having to refill his pint, she went back to the magazine.

"Directions, please."

Maxine squinted at him. Directions were not part of her job as temporary publican, at least not until Plant tore a page from her magazine, plunked his gold pen beside it and repeated his request.

She drew a few lines for roads and an X marking the lab. Then she gave him an evil look and shoved page and pen at him.

"Don't worry. I'll get you a subscription."

Wiggins had come back to say that Constable Pasco wasn't at the station and wasn't at home.

"Neither place?"

"Neither, sir."

Jury was silent for a moment. "Call the Selby C.I.D. See if they know where he is."

Polly shoved her glasses up on her head, as if that gave her a compass bearing. "But *why?* What makes you think Carrie would go there?"

"Because that's where she thinks someone took her terrier and I'm not going to sit around here arguing. No, not you," said Jury as Polly gathered up her coat.

"What do you *mean*, not me? I was here before either of you!"

"That makes a lot of sense," said Plant, buttoning his Chesterfield, picking up his stick. "We're not exactly queuing for a bus."

"It's a police matter, Polly," said Jury.

That made her drop the ugly glasses down over her eyes. "Then why're you taking *him?*"

Because I need him. But Jury didn't say that. He leaned over the table and gave Polly a wonderful smile. "Because if I leave him here with you, you'll have him in that Silver Ghost driving at eighty miles per out to that lab, dear Polly." He kissed her cheek.

Her glasses steamed up.

PART 6

An Amethyst remembrance

Is all I own—

Thirty

From a clump of bracken she had been watching the dark lab for an hour or more and wished she'd brought the binoculars, but it would have been too much to carry along with the torch and shotgun.

No one. At least no one had gone into the lab from her range of vision, so perhaps it wasn't tonight. Carrie got up from the ground, which was squelchy and cold, and walked toward the long building, dark except for one amber light inside. She couldn't understand that.

Of course the gate was locked, but the fence was easy enough to scale, and she did, dropping first the gun and then herself on the other side. The ammunition was in her pocket.

Because of the demonstrations, there had been talk of surrounding the whole building with barbed wire or electrifying the fence and getting a guard. The lab itself was hardly impregnable; if she couldn't get in by way of a door, she could by way of a window. Three of the doors needed keys to get in. But one small one at the end was padlocked. Joe Brindle hadn't been good for much, but he had taught her how to listen to the tumbler on a padlock, information he'd picked up from his safe-cracking days. *Acute hearing's what you got, girl*. She turned the knob, her ear close to the lock, and heard the nearly inaudible clicks. Carrie opened the door.

She had never come into this building, despite Fleming's invitations — again, she thought of Dr. Fleming. The staff were the only ones with keys, and whoever intended her to come here certainly must have a key, unless the person intended to break a window, not having had the benefit of Brindle's teaching. The single bulb at the other end of the corridor made a misty alley of light, showing rows of doors down both sides. The first ones were labeled "Restricted." Carrie turned her torch on one and tried the knob. It wasn't locked and she went inside.

What she found was an antiseptically clean room, with cats in separate cages, most of them asleep. A few were awake, or had come awake when the light swept over the cages and they sat up. The doors of the cages were mesh, and she went from one to another, looking in, putting her fingers through the mesh. Some of them backed away into the shelter of a dark corner; others clawed at the mesh. At least, she thought, they hadn't been declawed. The room was equipped with ultraviolet lights. Her hands took on a strange bluish glow. On the other side of the room were cats inside plastic bubbles. Carrie supposed by being in here she was contaminating the place.

There was a lightswitch on the wall, but she was afraid to turn it on; it might attract attention.

That was what she had found strange: the whole building should have been floodlit.

She loaded the gun and in her soundless sneakers made her way to the door, stiffbacked against the wall, peering as well as she could down the corridor. Not a sound.

She looked back at the cats in their cages. Carrie would have expected the yowlings and meowings of animals upset by a change in routine, if nothing else. But they were still silent. Blood tests, Dr. Fleming had said. Fifty percent of them would probably die, just to see how big a dose it would take to kill them.

One by one she opened the cages, being very quiet. It was almost as if the cats were cooperating, not letting whoever was in the building know where Carrie was. But it was really that they were scared, too scared to make a noise. The window was barred, but locked only with a simple latch. A high table beside the window she shoved beneath it. Then she peered down the corridor, still empty, stepped out, and closed the door.

In the next room were rabbits. On a long table she saw the harnesses. These weren't blood tests. Carrie knew what this was all about and she felt herself go cold. She thought she heard footsteps in the corridor, but she still inspected the rabbits. The harnesses were to keep their heads perfectly still, with little devices to hold their eyes open. So something could be sprayed into the eyes. That morning she had got soap in her eye, and the sting was terrible. But she could blink. She could dish cold water into it. The rabbits couldn't.

And where was Bingo, she wondered with growing terror, as the steps came closer. Carrie slowly raised the shotgun, stared at the rabbit whose eyes were so ravaged they looked like molten wax. The pain must have been unbearable. Her hands were shaking but she could still hold the butt to her shoulder as the steps came nearer. *Your Majesty* — she pretended to be addressing the Queen — *I think I'd call this the "termination condition."*

Carrie shot the rabbit.

From the doorway, a voice said, "Hold it right there, Carrie."

Pasco. *Constable Pasco.*

x

Jury switched the motor off far enough from the gate that he doubted anyone could have heard the car approaching.

"I don't believe it," said Melrose Plant. "I mean I *do*, but it's so —"

"It's so. And it was simple, really. Foolproof. A killer not even around when the victims die. Just scare the hell out of Una Quick, find out she's told Sally MacBride about that snapshot with the name 'Lister,' and Sally would probably have told Donaldson." Jury's smile was grim. " 'Probably.' Why the hell take chances? Una *did* muck about with the post." Jury hit the steering wheel. "Damn it! The post, the bloody post! It should have been so obvious."

"Hindsight always is. And as you said, anyone could have seen Carrie outside the Silver Vaults. And gone home with her. Or followed her home." He looked from the lab to Jury. *"Trompe l'oeil,* is that it?"

"That's it. You weren't at 'La Notre' that first day. Come on, let's get in there." They got out, walked across the squelchy ground. "God, you'd think Fleming would have floodlights on that place, wouldn't you?"

As they drew nearer, Jury saw the door on one end, the main door, and assumed there was probably one on the other end. "I'll take the door on one end, maybe you can go round to the other."

"I forgot my keys," said Melrose.

"Very funny. You don't know how to pick locks?"

They were in the process of hoisting themselves over the wall. "I can't *imagine,"* said Melrose, "invading the privacy of others in such a way."

In spite of everything, Jury smiled.

Thirty-one

And Constable Pasco knew how to use a handgun. He held it in both hands, crouching slightly. "Put it down!" he yelled.

"Where's Bingo?"

"I don't know about Bingo. Dammit, Carrie, I've had enough from you. I was driving from Selby. This place should have been lit up like Harrods at Christmas —"

The shot threw him twisting into the air. And then he fell, a dead weight in the corridor.

Carrie stared. *Constable Pasco.* She watched the blood slowly ooze through the back of his shirt and thought for one nightmare moment she must have fired.

Who was out there?

There were tiny steps that seemed to recede in the distance, running. Sweating, she reloaded the shotgun, switched off her torch, and did what she'd seen all the police do in those films she went to with the Baroness. Quickly, she stepped into the corridor and fired straight down it at a figure all in black — including a kind of ski-cap thing. The typical demonstrator.

Or someone pretending to be. It could have been anyone, and it disappeared into one of the rooms farther down the hall. Carrie ran into the next room, where dogs were barking.

But through the sound of the dogs she could hear breathing, fast breathing, and her name whispered.

There was no time to load up the shotgun, and she hoped the torch would blind whoever it was at least for a second or two when it fell on a figure in the corner. "Neahle!"

Neahle Meara was crouched down and crying, her hands fisted against her face.

Carrie went over to her. "Neahle, I might have killed you —" Neahle kept shaking and shaking her head, weeping soundlessly, quiet as the cats. Carrie knelt beside her and whispered, "How'd you get here? How'd you get in?"

"The door at the other end." She kept shaking her head until Carrie put her two hands on Neahle's own to make her stop. "Listen, we'll be still as mice. Okay? I'll sit here beside you." And she did, back flat against the cinder block. She whispered, "I've got this gun, Neahle. No one can do anything. Okay?"

Neahle had stopped the sobbing, was rubbing her eyes, and Carrie shut hers tightly, thinking only of the dead rabbit. And then shocked at herself for not thinking of Constable Pasco first. He was her friend, even if she pretended not. *God, please* — she stopped the thought; she did not believe in God.

Neahle was holding her hand. "I knew something bad was going to happen. I knew you were in trouble when —"

They both froze. The sound of other feet. But the feet stopped. And Carrie knew whoever was there had to look into each room. The gunfire hadn't given her away; it had confused the person coming down the corridor. Thank God it was a long one.

Carrie took out more ammunition, loaded the .412 again, and tightened her grip on Neahle's hand. "When what, Neahle?"

"The man from Scotland Yard. He had a picture of this place, but I was afraid they were looking for you. So I didn't tell them. I took the short-cut through the woods and ran all the way. I didn't tell." Neahle shook Carrie's arm. "Did I do wrong?"

She had steeled herself seven years ago against tears. Now the disappointment was overwhelming. If only Neahle *had* told him. "You did right."

Neahle put her head on Carrie's shoulder. Those footsteps were coming nearer. Neahle whispered, "We're going to get killed, aren't we, Carrie? And Bingo?"

"Anyone that walks through that door is going to get a hole blown in him a deer could jump through. You take the torch. When — I mean *if* the door opens, switch it on. It's a strong light, like hunters use."

Neahle merely nodded, looked down at the electric torch, back up at Carrie. "What if it's the wrong person that walks through?"

It was what Carrie needed. She started to giggle and clamped her hand over her mouth and so did Neahle, giggling too. *We're probably both going to die*, thought Carrie, *and we're laughing.*

"Neahle. Do you believe in God?"

"I guess." And then, disconsolately, "But, then, I'm Irish."

This made them clamp their hands to their mouths again and hang on to one another to keep from making any sound. They had to choke back the silliness. *Death*, thought Carrie, *is silly. It sure doesn't get you anywhere* — and she had to put her head down in spite of the steps coming closer to keep from laughing and it was Neahle who had to shake Carrie this time and tell her, *Listen!*

For there were other footsteps. Different.

Neahle was clearly frightened when Carrie stood up. Carrie heard her name spoken in a whisper.

It was a voice she would have known anywhere — Superintendent Jury's.

Who didn't know what he was walking into.

"Stay right there," said Carrie. "Quiet."

"Carrie?" said Neahle.

There was a small but mounting hysteria even in the one word. "You're all right, Neahle. *We're* all right."

"Carrie?" said Neahle.

Neahle didn't believe her. Carrie reached round her neck and undid the little clasp of the necklace. She dropped the necklace and amethyst ring into Neahle's hands. "Besides Bingo, this is what I like most. You know that. So hold on to it for me. Okay?" There was no logic in this, and Carrie knew it. But Neahle wouldn't. To her, it would be an icon, something to trust in.

The steps were muted but getting nearer. Carrie picked up the shotgun, simply held up the palm of her hand to Neahle's indrawn breath, and went toward the door.

She opened it a slot narrow as a penny. Superintendent Jury. No.

There was a sound from the other end of the corridor he was walking down.

No.

Carrie opened the door, butted the shotgun against her shoulder, and aimed at the figure halfway down the corridor.

"Carrie!" yelled Jury.

Carrie had lowered the gun because she couldn't understand why she was aiming the figure in black, now without the mask. Gillian Kendall.

And Gillian's handgun was trained not on her, but at Superintendent Jury.

No, thought Carrie, leaping in front of him.

☿

The shot caught her as it had Pasco. She looked up at Jury. "Neahle," Carrie pointed behind her.

But Gillian brought the gun up again. He said to Carrie, "Neahle will be okay. So will Bingo." Then he looked down the corridor. Ruth Lister.

"I'm pretty easily taken in, Ruth. Aren't I?"

Carrie's eyes were closed, but the lids fluttered. "Ruthie? The zoo ..." Her eyes closed again.

The zoo, Jury thought. "It was you who took Carrie. Of course, she would have gone with you."

Ruth Lister nodded, but her attention was wholly on the girl she thought she'd put paid to for the second time. Carrie was still breathing.

The gun moving slightly, she said to Carrie, "If you'll give me the necklace, love, I promise it'll all be over."

She was insane, thought Jury. How could it be over? How did she think she'd get away with this?

Torch the lab. Just another crazy demonstrator. Nothing but bones. And she'd have the little ring to prove that Carrie Fleet, Carolyn Lister, was dead. Whatever her story. She'd be capable of any story. A very plausible woman. Jury looked down at Carrie, whose eyes had opened again. She was smiling. There was only a bit of blood. . . . *For God's sake, Plant . . .*

"How'd you find Carrie, Ruth? I mean after you missed getting her from the Brindles? You wouldn't have taken the chance on presenting yourself to old Joe, surely, and asking her whereabouts?"

"Not as myself. But social services really *must* know where its charges are."

Jury kept Gillian talking. "You didn't simply end up in Ashdown by accident, did you?"

She laughed. "No. And I certainly wouldn't have pressed myself into service with the Baroness Regina. I was following Carrie. Did you know it was me, then? How?"

"Not until tonight. Not until I thought that the one person who had most to do with the post would be, of course, the secretary. You simply took the snapshot which the Brindles had sent with the letter out of the envelope."

"But Una had seen it first. And told Sally MacBride. Who *might* have told Donaldson. One has to cover all bases."

Jury felt blood oozing through his fingers. "How did you know Una Quick had told Sally MacBride?"

She smiled slightly, shaking her head. "Richard. You think things are so complicated. I merely asked her. Called her on the Monday night and threatened her. Actually, I hoped that would finish the job, but to make sure, I told her to be at that call box on Tuesday. Richard, this is fascinating, but I can't believe you came alone."

"Wiggins is trying to get ahold of Paul Fleming."

"Well. My little affair with Paul at least got me a key to the lab and the drug to give Grimsdale's hounds. It took some working out, you see. I knew that getting Carrie's dog here was the way to get *her* here."

From the shadows at the other end of the hall Jury at last saw the shape of Melrose Plant emerge. *Took you long enough.* It was the ragged breathing of Carrie Fleet that enraged him. More than this woman who had led him right up the garden.

"And the other animals —?"

The safety on the gun snicked back. "I suppose I owe you something. Another minute, perhaps."

Carrie Fleet groaned and raised her hand to ward off whatever devils were forming in her semiconscious state. "No."

Gillian said, "Red herrings, Richard. Easy enough to dose the cat up with aspirin — which is, incidentally, what I took tonight. Not a sedative."

"It was a convincing act. Hysteria, the works." He watched as Plant got closer, moving in total silence. "Do you know how much you look like Carrie? The perfect profiles. The first day at 'La Notre,' I should have seen it. Like seeing double."

"Bingo," said Carrie.

"The damned dog's all right. He's in the last room down the corridor." She raised the gun up and brought it down. "About you, Richard, I'm truly sorry." She smiled.

Melrose was behind her. "Mind dropping that?"

Ruth Lister laughed. "Lord Ardry. *Not* Sergeant Wiggins." She paled, but kept the gun steady. "Knowing you, I doubt very much that's a gun at my back."

"It isn't."

Jury watched her expression turn from a ghastly smile to a blindfold look. She seemed to stand stock still for a long time. And then she dropped like a stone.

Melrose pulled the swordstick from her back and let it clatter to the floor.

Then he went into a room at his right and came out with the terrier, Bingo, which he put on the floor beside Carrie.

Jury called Neahle's name and she came running from her hiding place in a room down the corridor. He wanted to tell her that things were all right.

Things were not.

Jury was holding Carrie in his arms, his head against her silver hair, his hands sticky with blood.

There was blood everywhere. Pasco. Gillian. It snaked down the corridor.

Neahle was wild-eyed. Slowly, she bent down, then simply lay across Carrie, who said, "Got the ring?"

The dark brown head was close to the silvery-blond one. "I got the ring, Carrie."

Carrie Fleet held out her hand, now strangely transparent, for the necklace. Its reflection in the weird amber light turned her blood almost to gold.

⚮

Melrose Plant remembered that shape coming out of the fog, passing from kennel to kennel.

She said to Neahle, "It might be worth something, this ring. Maybe the Baroness would help . . ."

Carrie's head fell on Jury's shoulder. "Sanctuary."

The Past is such a curious Creature
  To look her in the Face
A Transport may reward us
  Or a Disgrace —

Unarmed if any meet her
  I charge him fly
Her rusty Ammunition
  Might yet reply.

—Emily Dickinson